DRAGON SLAYER

THE LEGEND OF ST. GEORGE

AN ORIGINAL SCREENPLAY BY

STEPHEN JAGER

ISBN: 9781727381436
Independently published

"They followed worthless idols
and themselves became worthless."

2 Kings 17:15

- Holy Bible

The face of a beautiful young woman in her early 20s.

Her eyes are closed.

Perspiration sparkles on her trembling skin.

Her quivering lips slightly parted.

A decorative wreath adorns her head.

Her long red hair waterfalls down onto her shoulders.

A long white dress with gold trim, drapes down to her feet.

Her breathing stirs her garment.

Her toes nervously curl into the sand.

EXT. THE LAKE OF SILENE - DAY

The young woman stands on the small beach at the edge of a modest

LAKE

TITLE CARD: THE LAKE OF SILENE

At one end, an imposing slice of rock, like some giant arm, juts out over the lake to almost its third.

Beside it a narrow river pours its continuance into the lake.

1

The woman's breathing accelerates causing her to shut her eyes even tighter.

A rope is tied around her waist which in turn is tied to an adorned...

STAKE

Securely stuck in the ground behind her.

Her toes nervously dig deeper into the coarse pebbly sand.

We hear the sound of the water being stirred near her. As if someone, or something, is breaking the surface.

The woman swallows harder and more frequently. Her hands grab the rope around her waist. She tugs at it.

The sound grows louder.

The woman pulls harder at the rope. Her stance becoming increasingly uncomfortable.

Her lips move more rapidly as she recites a chant from memory...

The sound of gushing water louder as if something large has risen from the deep...

Rising in front of her as is evident of the growing shadow against her dress, towering beyond her height, until it

completely blocks out the sun.
Her chant shrivels to a whimper.

Her eyes fly wide open...

as does her mouth...

Black.

Her scream dies at birth.

EXT. LAKE OF SILENE - CONTINUOUS

The Lake is quiet.

Smooth as the sky above it.

A thin layer of mist hovers just above
the water in a gentle caress.

On the deserted beach stands only...

THE STAKE

A ribbon clings to it, until it simply
falls.

One end of the rope is still tied to
the stake.

The other end lies lifeless and shredded
in a pool of blood, vanishing its seep
into the sand.

The mist drifts in from the lake, across
the sand, towards the surrounding bush
and multiplies up the steep embankment.

At the top, a crooked road winds towards a series of man-made structures a short distance away - A VILLAGE.

EXT. VILLAGE OF SILENE - CONTINUOUS

Trails of smoke zigzag quietly into the air.

A simple patchwork of wood and stone buildings surrounds a large central square.

TITLE CARD: SILENE

The atmosphere is quiet and somber.

A few inhabitants are dotted throughout the streets and square. Their faces hard - like they've seen too much pain already.

One particular building stands at the edge of the square.

Larger than all the rest, it is marked by two carved stone pillars on either side of the entrance - THE TEMPLE

INT. THE TEMPLE OF JUTURNA - CONTINUOUS

The interior is dark and smoky. The only light flickers from the dimly lit torches mounted in wrought-iron on the stone walls.

Shadows, like giant stilt-walkers, crisscross on the far side of the temple wall.

BLASIUS, 60s, a fiercely creased, bony man in a black robe. From his skull cap with ear coverings hanging all the way down to his thighs, determines him the priest.

In his hands he waves a smoking branch in front of an enormous floor-to-roof statue of a woman carved out of stone.

TITLE CARD: JUTURNA - goddess of fountains, wells and springs. Her jewelry inlaid with jade and gold.

A loud voice thunders from the entrance somewhere behind the priest Blasius.

ALBUS (O.S.)
Juturna...!

Blasius turns stoically to face...

LORD ALBUS (50s)

A thick-set man with a stern face. Albus throws the idol Juturna, a piercing and altogether disapproving look.

Blasius bows deep and piously in front of Lord Albus.

ALBUS
...hears us not.

Blasius stiffens. His fiery black eyes a
veil to his superciliousness.

BLASIUS
Lord Albus. I caution you not to
provoke the gods.

Albus does not shift his challenging
gaze from Juturna.

ALBUS
Our lady, remains silent.

A beautifully dark young woman, SABRA
(20s), with long thick black hair,
appears from the shadows behind Albus.

She stops beside her father. He
immediately softens at her presence.

ALBUS
What if it were your daughter?

Blasius keeps his eyes fixed on Sabra,
as if they share a secret.

BLASIUS
The lots are drawn.

Albus suddenly grabs the arm of
Blasius.

ALBUS
What if it were your daughter?!

Blasius looks down at Albus's hand with
increased contempt.

BLASIUS
All are daughters of Silene. Juturna is
not cruel.

ALBUS
No.

But we are.

Albus angrily let's go of Blasius's
arm. Sabra interjects - spirited as a
young lioness.

SABRA
It is the will of our lady Father. I am
ready.

Albus looks at his daughter as if no
longer recognizing her.

ALBUS
How can this be?

BLASIUS
Their sacrifice does not go unnoticed.

Albus cocks his head with disbelief.

Sabra immediately puts her hand on his
arm as if to abate his temper.

ALBUS
Not cruel?!

His voice on the verge of breaking.

ALBUS
Open your eyes Blasius!

His arm points outwards, somewhere in the direction of the lake.

ALBUS
That... that thing!
Is a scourge!

Albus touches his daughters hand as he breaks.

ALBUS
Who will rid us of it?!

EXT. TOWN - DAY

A large sprawling town characterized by its taller buildings, undoubtedly well on its way to becoming a city. It bustles with activity as pedestrians weave between horses and horse-drawn carts.

A scruffy building comes into view, drunkenly leaning against its neighbor. A wooden sign dangles precariously off a single rusted chain. The sign reads...

BLACK TAVERN

INT. BLACK TAVERN - CONTINUOUS

Eagerly the morning sun streams in past the wooden shutters. A few drunkards like vampires keep to the shadowy corners.

The proprietor behind the bar coughs and follows with a hearty, unearthly clearing of his throat.

The tavern doors suddenly smash open as if ruckussed by a sudden storm.

GNAEUS (40s), A bulbous man not befitting his well-spruced and stylish attire, storms in, flanked by his two equally fat associates.

Huffing and puffing like an angry young bull, Gnaeus barks at the man behind the bar.

GNAEUS
Where is he?!

The proprietor looks over the counter, down at the floor.

Gnaeus follows the proprietor's eyes to

TWO FEET

sticking out from underneath a table.

The proprietor throws an empty beaker at the feet.

The feet don't move.

One of Gnaeus's associates kicks over the table, revealing a...

MAN

flat on his back sprawled out of the floor. His unsheathed sword by his side.

GEORGE (30s) handsomely coarse, unshaven - and passed out.

Gnaeus grabs a patron's half full beaker off the nearest table and pours it over George's face.

George immediately sits up with a sputter.

But just as quickly falls back down grabbing his groaning hungover head.

Gnaeus, still with the empty beaker in his hand, drops the pewter vessel onto George's crotch.

This time George bolts upright and projects a vomit straight onto Gnaeus's pretty buckled shoes.

Gnaeus turns volcano red.

GNAEUS
What do I pay you for!?

With the help of his sword, George stands with difficulty. He sways as if an anvil is strapped to his back.

His attire, in contrast to Gnaeus's, is dull, dirty and threadbare. He fondles his pockets.

GEORGE
You pay me to drink.

He pulls out his leather money purse.
Turns it upside down - empty.

GEORGE
Obviously not enough.

While George carefully puts away his
detumescent purse, Gnaeus and his two
associates bend backwards; evidently
repulsed by the foul stench clinging to
the rogue.

George stumbles past them and makes for
the tavern doors.

EXT. BLACK TAVERN - CONTINUOUS

Bursting through the well-weathered
doors, George immediately shields his
eyes from the sun - a hammer to his
hangover.

With Gnaeus like a battered kettle
against his heel, George stumbles
towards the crossbar purposed to tie up
horses.

GNAEUS
You've lost them haven't you?!

George stops beside a...

SPEAR

...firmly stuck in the ground next to
the horse-dock.

Around the top of the spear dangles what
looks like the remains of his horse's
reins.

He grabs the end that's been chewed off
and roars as he looks up and down the
street.

GEORGE
Where's that coward of a donkey?!

GNAEUS
What do I pay you for?! I've tolerated
your...your...

GEORGE
Insolence!

GNAEUS
Inconsistency!

George makes for the horses' water
trough.

GNAEUS
...no, make that plural...
inconsistencies for long enough. Do you
hear me?!

George plunges his head in the water.
From inside the trough Gnaeus's rant is
reduced to a mere muffle.

Gnaeus frowns. Associate One moves
towards George but Gnaeus stops him.

GNAEUS
I want him to be sprightly as he can be
when you take his tooth.

Seconds pass. Seconds turn to minutes.
George's head remains in the trough.

Gnaeus goes back inside the tavern and
returns with a chair. Sits down.

Associate One looks at Associate Two
and frowns.

ASSOCIATE TWO
Maybe he'll drown himself.

Associate Two folds his arms and leans
against the tavern wall.

George eventually pulls his head from
the trough. His breathing heavy.

Gnaeus jumps at the suddenness almost
sliding off his chair. For this, he
stands even angrier.

George and Gnaeus nose to nose.

GNAEUS
Did I not ex-pli-cit-ly say...to keep
an eye--

GEORGE
Wish way?

GNAEUS
Where is your horse?

George throws a menacing glance at
Gnaeus's two associates.

GEORGE
You have more than one pair of eyes

Gnaeus. Which way?

Gnaeus points left.

GNAEUS
They headed north.

George smirks as if he doesn't believe
Gnaeus.

Turns to pull his spear from the ground
and begins his run in the opposite
direction of Gnaeus' finger.

Gnaeus frowns and shouts after George.

GNAEUS
I said north!

Gnaeus turns to his associates and
growls.

GNAEUS
What is wrong with him?!

EXT. WOODS - DAY

Above: the sunlight blinks through the
trees.

Wish-wish-wish - we hear a running man.

Hush-hush-hush - we hear is breathing.

Below: We see George running down the
roughly cut road through the woods,
spear in hand.

Some distance behind him: Gnaeus and
his two others following on horses.

George suddenly stops to look down at
the horse-hoof prints in the mud. He
touches them before looking right down
into the denser woods.

Smiles, and with a spirited sprint
disappears into trees.

Gnaeus stops at the same spot George
had. Peering right he catches just a
glimpse of the disappearing George.

Associates One and Two halt either side
of Gnaeus.

ASSOCIATE ONE
How does he know?

GNAEUS
He's a soldier.

ASSOCIATE TWO
You mean deserter.

Gnaeus kicks his horse into the woods.

Associates follow.

INT. WOODS - DAY

Three hard looking men stand around the
remainder of their fire. Their three
disheveled horses nearby.

TOOTHLESS - The ugliest of the three, kicks sand over the fire.

CUTLASS - the biggest, stares into a large sack of gold. He smiles before throwing it onto his horse and re-tying it.

RUTHLESS - the fiercest and most emaciated of the three, is the first to get on his horse.

The other two follow in quick succession.

Whoop-whoop-whoop - the sound of a traveling spear.

Ruthless has just enough time to widen his eyes as the spear cuts through his collar and rips him clean off his horse to pin him onto a tree.

Cutlass, sees an already airborne George, who kicks him clean off his horse, to take his place in his own saddle.

Toothless, on the horse beside, swings his sword wildly at George who neatly slide sideways around, and off the saddle to land underneath the horse.

From underneath the animal George grabs Toothless's leg, and with an almighty downward pull, cracks Toothless's face on the saddle of the horse above him, he had just occupied, tumbling the crook down to the soggy ground.

Cutlass stumbles to his feet clutching his chest with one hand and sword in the other. He charges George, who already armed with a rock, hurls it at him.

Cutlass instinctively tries to protect himself from the flying rock with his own sword.

The rock however, bangs straight into the flat side of his sword, which in turn bangs straight into his own nose, breaking it, which drops him like a screaming bag of gold.

Back to the first man against the tree, Ruthless squirms as he loosens himself by tearing his collar and drops to the ground...

...only to be yanked up and dragged the short distance towards his other two cohorts squirming on the ground.

George pulls his spear free from the tree and upon turning, meets the arrival of Gnaeus and his entourage of two.

Mildly stunned, Gnaeus and his two henchmen watch George pull the three bags of gold from the thieves' horses.

Drops it at the hoof of Gnaeus's horse.

Associate One and Two dismount to load up the bags onto their own horses.

Gnaeus takes out three coins and tosses it to George. It bounces off his abdomen and falls down to his shoes.

George's smirk changes to a more concerned frown.

He picks up the coins and rolls it around in his hand before giving Gnaeus a sneer of dissatisfaction.

GNAEUS
They've robbed every town south of Nicomedia. You were supposed to watch them so we could catch them red-handed.

ASSOCIATE ONE
Where are the other four?

GNAEUS
Precisely. What of the others?

Associate Two adds unnecessarily.

ASSOCIATE ONE
There were seven.

GEORGE
Well I would need seven pairs of eyes then...

Turns angrily towards the nearest horse and mumbles.

GEORGE
...and a lot more beer.

Gnaeus, in his supposed benevolence, tosses a fourth coin against the back of George's head.

GNAEUS
Dispose of them.

George turns to look down at the fourth
coin at his feet.

GEORGE
I relieve myself... from my post.

He looks and Gnaeus and courtesies with
a flourish before turning back to the
horse without picking up the coin.

It is evident from George's clenched
teeth that a thunderstorm is brewing
inside of him. George grabs the saddle,
about to mount, when he hears..

ASSOCIATE TWO
Once a deserter always a deserter.

George smiles even though he doesn't
want to and whispers menacingly to
himself.

GEORGE
Dessert. A sweet course eaten at the
end of a meal. There's always a chance
Georgie, the gawk cannot spell.

Associate One and Two both crack their
knuckles.

GEORGE
Run Georgie. Run.

George abandons the horse and walks
towards the three thieves, gathering
their littered weapons along the way.

To the sudden horror of Gnaeus and his
consorts, he drops the weaponry at the
feet of the captured.

They sit up a little straighter, whilst
George quickly addresses them.

GEORGE
I find myself without occupation.

With their uncertainty diminishing,
Less and Lass look at each other as
George concludes.

GEORGE
They're not armed.

Gnaeus's eyes bulge as he tries to turn
his horse but the reigns are already in
the hands of Toothless. Three on three
as the thieves try and pull Gnaeus and
his men off their horses.

George hijacks himself one of the
thieves horses whilst Cutlass pulls
Associate One off his horse, just
as Associate Two manages a kick to
Ruthless's head.

Gnaeus kicks Toothless on the head and
shouts to George.

GNAEUS
Alright!

George ambles his horse a little closer,
the thieves stiffen at the sudden
prospect of negotiation.

GNAEUS
Double!

TOOTHLESS
Half!

George looks down at the thief and
smiles.

GNAEUS
Half and one!

And with that Gnaeus tosses George two
bags.

Toothless's eyes bulge. Throwing up
Gnaeus's reins he barks like a hoarse
pirate.

TOOTHLESS
Take it all!

He runs. Consorts follow.

George empties half the second bag onto
the ground.

Gnaeus bumps his horse forward into
George's and hisses.

GNAEUS
Mark me. I will find you! And I shall
bring a horde!

GEORGE
You don't have enough gold Gnaeus.

George turns his horse and pursues.

EXT. WOODS - SECONDS LATER

Toothless runs at full tilt. George
trots his horse calmly into view, right
beside the thief.

Toothless, surprised, turns to face
George while he runs and kicks himself
out stone cold against a tree.

EXT. LAKE - DAY

George looks out pensively over the
lake.

Next to him, on their knees with hands
tied behind their backs execution style,
the three thieves.

George moves his gaze around the lake's
edges.

TOOTHLESS (O.S.)
Let us go...

His gaze stops on the ruffian.

TOOTHLESS
...and we'll go easy on you.

George ponders the man before cutting
him free from his ropes.

Toothless stands, a little surprised
but smiles nonetheless, rubbing his
wrists.

TOOTHLESS
You're a very wise man indeed.

George gives his surroundings one last
scan before thrusting his sword into
the ground.

Throws a glance at the remaining two.

GEORGE
I'll be right back.

George suddenly grabs Toothless by the
back of his shirt and drags him into the
water amidst a barrage of protestations
and declensions.

Once thigh-high George stops and roughly
straightens the bewildered man back on
his feet.

Faces him square on. Toothless shakes,
expecting the worst.

GEORGE
Are you repentant of your sins?

Toothless pulls his best muddled
toothless face.

GEORGE
Are you repentant of your sins?

TOOTHLESS
What?!

George fumbles around his own neck, his
hand slipping inside his tunic he pulls
out an...

IRON CROSS.

GEORGE
You take from people what is not yours.
Rich people. Doesn't make it right. Are
you remorseful of the life that may
have been thrust upon you?

Toothless the opportunist, answers
deadpan.

TOOTHLESS
Yes. I am...that word...indeed.

GEORGE
Then you are forgiven.

In another sudden movement, George grabs
him by his clothes, kicks his feet from
out under him and pushes him underneath
the water.

Toothless's arms flail, splashing
violently as he no doubt thinks he's
being drowned.

GEORGE
I baptize you in the name of the
Father, His Son and the Holy Ghost.

George pulls him back up. Toothless
sputters up water, evidently with no
time to hold his breath, swallowed some.

GEORGE
Congratulations. You are free to begin
your new life.

George ends with a flourish of his wrist, whilst Toothless returns his stupefied expression.

GEORGE
See you on the other side.

Toothless runs back to shore.
George turns to follow but quickly stops when he sees...

On the shore of the lake...

SEVEN MEN

The full company of thieves, and no doubt amongst them, murderers.

Toothless turns and smiles menacingly at George. Lifts his hand and beckons for George to come closer.

George's hand instinctive travels up to his now empty scabbard.

His eyes fixes his sword, still stuck in the sand.

EXT. LAKE - MINUTES LATER

Toothless pushes George's head underneath the water.
He cackles with laughter while his cadre mills on shore dividing the gold from George's bag.

Toothless lifts George's head and
hisses.

TOOTHLESS
See you on the other side.

His spit landing on George's cheeks
before thrusting George's head one final
time into the water.

Holds it there.

Frowns at the fact that George doesn't
struggle to get free.

As if he's resigned himself to death.

EXT. HOUSE - DAY - FLASHBACK BEGINS

-- In the distance, a large stone house
stands proud in the center of a green
estate.

-- The window frames are large and
ornate.

-- The courtyard behind the house boasts
a large fountain.

-- From the furnishing we gather; not
too wealthy. Definitely not poor.

-- Apparel and bedsheets drift
melancholically down from an open
window.

-- Everything is inaudible and slow.

-- Looking into the top window, we see
two men push a screaming middle-aged
woman down onto the bed.

-- From the next window falls a chair.
It unravels onto the paving below.

-- Servants run from the house, terror-
stricken, pursued by men with swords.

-- A middle-aged man, already wounded,
kneels in front of his son, GEORGE
(14), and shouts something at him.

-- George looks up past his father at
the men approaching.

-- Urged by his father, George turns
and runs.

-- Looking back he sees

A LOOTER

Run his sword through his father's
spine.

-- George stops to scream, his face
contorts with the immensity of what he
is witnessing.

-- The looters notices the boy and
pursue.

-- Again, George turns to run.

-- Running down the dark entrance to
the courtyard, George stumbles out into

the sunlight, the fountain right in
front of him.

-- On her back, floating in the waters
of the fountain, lies

HIS MOTHER

-- George's mouth opens as if to swallow
the world.

-- Moments later, two looters burst out
into the courtyard. Looking left and
right sees that George has vanished.
They immediately split up, each of them
running down the side corridors.

-- The Fountain - water-lilies dot its
surface.

-- In amongst the floating plants,
reveals George - completely submerged.

-- Underneath his mother. With his arms
around her. His whisper, echoes inside
his head.

GEORGE
Mother.

Wake up.

FLASHBACK ENDS

EXT. LAKE - DAY

-- George lies face down, floating in the water. The edge of the lake deserted. Toothless and his band of thieves long gone.

-- Inside the water: George stares into the blackness. He hears the voice of his mother, like a distant echo.

MOTHER (O.S.)
George. Wake up.

-- He stirs. Lifts himself out from the water and stands.

-- Gulps down deep breaths.

-- Collapses down on his back on the shore of the lake, arms wide.

-- A large chunky black horse, ASHKELON, appears above him. At first sniffs and then snuffles George.

Then, as if suddenly repulsed by the pestilential miasma of his rider, snobbishly snorts himself away.

GEORGE
Where have you been Ashkelon?

EXT. TAVERN - NIGHT

The silhouette and lights of a quaint little tavern nestled in the woods comes into view.

The sign, barely legible reads

THE WHITE HORSE INN

The crickets crick-crick to a dreary
old folk tune in minors emanating from
the Inn.

INT. THE WHITE HORSE INN - CONTINUOUS

The interior is misty, musty and dour.
Patrons huddle over the drinks and food.

Shadows glide against the wall behind
the bard with his lyre.

He sings...

"The mist ghosts in,
stings bones with cold.
The forests bristle,
with voices of old.

From ash to dust,
high is the cost.
But the fires still burn,
for the lost."

George sits in the corner, swaying
above his drink, listening to the song.

"The spear is hidden
in the flood.
So are the cries,
the thieves of our blood.

Cursing their bondage,
from their fiery frost.
Whilst the fires still burn,
for the lost."

George swallows the contents of his
beaker.

A woman sits down in front of him. Her
marble breasts half exposed. George
shakes his head.

GEORGE
I can't.

Pulls out his iron cross to show her.
His words slurring with the shake of
his head.

GEORGE
This is my new life. I won't.

The woman smiles sympathetically at him.
She takes his cross and gently places
it back inside his tunic, out of sight.

Takes his hand. George's face contorts
with pain from buried memories, but
stands willingly.

She leads him upstairs.

INT. THE TEMPLE OF JUTURNA - NIGHT -
CONTINUOUS

Sabra on her knees in front of the
statue of the goddess Juturna. Her

hands clasped together in prayer. Her
expression stoic. Confident. Stony.

She closes her eyes.
INT. THE WHITE HORSE INN - CONTINUOUS

The young woman sits in front of George
on the bed beside him.

Her eyes closed.

With a piece of cloth, George blindfolds
her.

Kisses her.

The bard's music ends.

"...the fires still burn for the lost."

EXT. THE WHITE HORSE INN - DAY

The sunlight blinks through the trees.
Crickets have turned into cheeping,
twittering birds.

A number of horses stand tied-up out
the front.

George's horse, even though blindfolded,
still manages to chew his reigns.

Success! The reigns splits in half.

Ashkelon then proceeds to run his face
up and down against the crossbar to try
and remove the blindfold. In this he
also succeeds.

Steps backwards and snorts with
satisfaction.

The tavern door flies open and George,
as is customary, stumbles outside. He
squints and tries his best to shield his
eyes from the light, whilst he zigzags
towards his horse.

Grabbing his saddle prompts Ashkelon to
sniff his master and immediately shorts
in disgust.

George is visibly angry.

GEORGE
Not this again!

He cups his hand over his mouth to smell
his own breath, leaving Ashkelon to
hurry away. George throws up his hand.

GEORGE
Stop!

Ashkelon does. George wavers towards
his black steed, quickly lunging for
the reigns.

GEORGE
What? You're too good for me now?

George leans in closer and hisses.

GEORGE
I see your disdain. Cut it out or I'll
cut off your hair. Don't think I won't
do it, you mule.

George puts his foot in the stirrup
when Ashkelon abruptly lunges
forward,knocking George backwards.

George looks up at his one foot now
stuck in his stirrup before Ashkelon
continues his forward march into the
woods dragging his master along through
the brush.

Arms swinging George shouts.

GEORGE
Stoooop!

Ashkelon however, continues, weaving
between the trees. A screaming George
dangling from one stirrup, his head and
back gathering mud and leaves.

Eventually Ashkelon stops. George still
hanging from his boot, shouts.

GEORGE
That's it! I'm selling, no giving you,
to the butchers, you corrupt excuse for
a horse! You are meat Ash! You hear
me?! Meat!

George strains upwards to grab hold
of the stirrup when his eyes suddenly
bulge.

GEORGE
Ashkelon? No!

Ashkelon steps into - A RIVER - pulling
George into the water with him.

George slips out his boot and lands in the water. Goes under before bopping back up. Angrier.

GEORGE
Meat!

As he punches the water he loses his footing and falls back over. But this time the river grabs him, holds him and ever so gently pushes him along.

GEORGE
See what you've done!

Ashkelon's ears straighten themselves with worry as he watches George float away from him in the current.

George's shout growing fainter.

GEORGE
You better run Ashkelon! You hear me? You'd better run, you illiterate ass!

A horse with a conscience, Ashkelon trots along the bank of the river after George, who floats further and further away.

EXT. LAKE OF SILENE - DAY

The sacrificial stake.

The priest Blasius ties the rope firmly around it. He turns to look at the beauty that is Sabra.

In front of her stands her father,
looking down at her hands in his he sees
them tremble. Letting go he realizes
that it is his own hands palpitating.
Hers are as calm as the lake's waters
behind him.

Sabra attempts to alleviate the agony
infecting her father's entire demeanor.

SABRA
Be happy for me Father. Perhaps my
blood will be enough--

He interrupts her.

ALBUS
There is a man!

She frowns.

ALBUS
His disciples say... He came back from
the dead. They saw him die!--

SABRA
Father--

Blasius, overhearing, accelerates his
shuffle closer. Albus's sanity is on the
brink.

ALBUS
They say He is a God! The one true God!

BLASIUS (O.S.)
Rumors!

Blasius sneers as he puts the rope
around Sabra's waist.

BLASIUS
Blasphemous rumors!

Gently she puts her hands on the
priest's - declining to be tied. Blasius
nods and drops the rope.

Sabra wipes the tears streaming down
his desperate cheeks.

ALBUS
He has a name. Just like you have
a name Sabra. All we need to do is
believe.

And still Sabra meets his exhortation
with gentle confidence.

SABRA
We serve the goddess. We always have.
We always will.

Blasius smiles triumphantly as he
piously retreats, waving his smoky
branch.

A few villagers stand at a distance,
having gathered for the spectacle.
Albus sees them, and drawing his sword
storms them.

ALBUS
Half my land!

The villagers scurry like rats.

ALBUS
You will not take half my land but
you will spectate! You will watch my
daughter die?!

The last of the villagers disappear.
Albus stops and drops his head. Inhales
before putting his sword away. Turns to
face his daughter and from a distance
tries his best to match her confidence.
The muscle in his jaw pulsates at the
sight of the priest, standing between
him and Sabra.

Blasius raises his arms.

BLASIUS
Oh great Juturna. Keeper of springs of
life. We humbly appease your servant of
the lake.

Sabra stares out over the small misty
lake. Her arms drift up either side of
her. Her eyes flutter as if a trance
injects her. And with that her eyelids
close.

Blasius's voice drones behind her. Her
lips move in her own private exhortation
to Juturna.

She hears the water stir in front of
her.

The unexpected fear of death grapples
her and Sabra swallows.

A shadow grows on her.

She suddenly hears...

A COUGH AND SPUTTER.

Sabra's eyes fly open and she immediately
shrieks.

Blasius grabs his heart and
involuntarily steps backward.

Albus's head jumps forward to keep his
eyeballs from falling from his face.

In front of Sabra stands...

GEORGE.

Drenched and covered with lake debris
resembling ribbons of weed.

Sabra's mouth opens. She brings her arms
close to her chest, tries to decipher
an appropriate response.

George looks curiously at her attire.
Then leans sideways to inspect the
sacrificial stake behind her.
Leaning the opposite way, he notes then
the two men spaced out behind her. All
sundry like comical frozen statuettes.

George puts his little finger in his ear
and wiggles it to try and dislodge the
water.

Keeping his eyes on Sabra, he hops on
one leg to try and flush out the water.
Sabra, still utterly shocked keeps her

eyes on him. Her head nodding with his bounce.

Blasius blinks and eventually shuffles forward. Albus follows and draws his sword.

George notices Albus approaching with a weapon and feels for his own, but once again - an empty scabbard.

George shrugs and brings up his fists.

Albus and Blasius halt.

George smiles, happy that his fists are scarier than Albus's sword. He gives them a look just to make certain.

Sabra's eyes grow whiter as she starts shaking.

George is suddenly perturbed that his fists are really scaring her.

But she is no longer looking at him.

George sees a shadow grow on the sand around him, over himself and Sabra in front of him. Albus and Blasius once again retreating - fast.

Fists back up, George swings around to face...

THE DRAGON

His jaw drops at the frightful sight:

-- Like a giant prehistoric lizard, the grey reddish beast stands poised like a cobra. Roughly the size of a large horse, yet supremely formidable on its two back legs.

-- Its lizard-like tail doubles the length of its body.

-- Its reptilian skin armored with overlapping diamond-shaped scales.

-- On it's back are spread two large bat-like wings. A beautifully distressed web of cartilage, bone and skin.

-- From the tip of its tail to the top of its head, runs a ridge of spikes, arranged like broken and infected teeth.

-- Resembling miniature elephant tusks, five hazardous claws on each leg.

-- But fiercest of all, its face; Alien-like tentacles randomly grow and contract from the skin that surrounds its mouth; quivering teeth as numerous as that of a shark, yet boasting the addition of two sets of saber-sized tusks.

-- Two angry, alien-crazed, liquid-black eyes, sits below two scarred and scuffed embattled horns.

-- Akin to an eel its slimy, slivery forked tongue slithers between its teeth as if a ravenous hunter.

-- Saliva drips like elastic poison, slower than the water that gushes like miniature waterfalls from places between its scales.

Without a moment's hesitation, George bolts, running away, down the sand as fast as he can.

However, he makes the fatal error of peering over his shoulder. He sees Sabra close her eyes. She moves her arms away from her sides, as a sign that she's ready to be taken.

The Dragon steps towards her. George stops.

GEORGE
What are you doing?!

He sees the two men retreat which make him seethe.

GEORGE
Run Georgie! Run!

Growls like a naughty kid being asked to clean his room.

GEORGE
Aargh!

Sabra's body shakes as the Dragon moves even closer towards her.

Its wings spread out as far out as it can, the beast readies itself to devour the beauty.

Albus stands frozen still with the sword in his hand when George snatches it from him as he sprints by.

The Dragon snaps his jaws towards her just as...

George dives her out of harm's way.

THE DRAGON EATS DIRT.

Back on his feet George hurls the sword cowardly at the Dragon. The sword's handle bounces off the Dragon's forehead.

The Dragon roars with an underlying and piercing alien screech. Sand drains from its mouth as it watches George dragging Sabra towards the trees at side end of the beach.

The Dragon goes down on all fours and pursues, its body zigzagging like that of a prehistoric alligator.

SABRA
What are you doing?!

Sabra wrestles herself free from George's grip.

GEORGE
What does it look like I'm doing??

SABRA
You have no idea what's going on here do you?!

Sabra turns to move towards the dragon.
George's mouth once again falls opens.
He instinctively grabs her around the
waist and drags her back to the trees.

SABRA
Let me go!

The Dragon accelerates. Blasius and
Albus, spectate in a state of shock.

SABRA
You're making her angry!

GEORGE
Oh it already looks angry to me
princess.

She bends down and bites his hand. With
a bellow he lets her go. Sabra then
turns and boots him full in the chest.
He falls backwards in the sand just as
the Dragon swoops on her.

The Dragon folds one of its wings over
Sabra, lifts and neatly rolls her
inside.

Then with one of its front feet, pins
George to the sand, its claw firmly
on his chest. With a spine-chilling
caterwaul twists its jaws towards
George.

GEORGE'S IRON CROSS SLIPS OUT ABOVE HIS
SHIRT.

THE SUN REFLECTS ITS SHAPE, RIGHT INTO
THE BLACK EYES OF THE DRAGON.

A MOMENTARY FLASH OF BLINDNESS, IS
ENOUGH TO REPEL THE VAMPIRIC ATTRACTION.

Bolting backwards, the Dragon drops
Sabra onto the sand.

Like a wounded hyena, it hisses, before
scurrying back into the water like a
dog with its tail between its legs.

None more surprised than George.
Twirling his iron cross between his
fingers, he stands frowning. Quickly
drops it back behind his garments as
Sabra storms him.

SABRA
What did you do?!

GEORGE
You want to be eaten?!

She pushes him as he retreats.

SABRA
What did you do?!

GEORGE
You first.

SABRA
Do you know what you've done?!

GEORGE
You're like an echo.

Sabra suddenly fearful looks up at the
sky while George smells his clothes.

SABRA
You've angered the goddess.

Sabra turns and briskly walks off to get
away from him. George shakes his head.

GEORGE
Must have been my breath.

Blasius and Albus watch George following
Sabra. The spectacle unfolding they are
still uncertain how to react.

SABRA
Get away from me!

George looks at the sky.

GEORGE
Why? Afraid that your god will send a
bolt of lightning?

Sabra turns to face him and hisses. She
points at the lake.

SABRA
The goddess Juturna will curse you.

George throws up his arms.

GEORGE
Of course. A woman.

SABRA
No, she will curse us for angering her
servant!

George puts his hands on his hips and
utters smugly, as if he's just had an
epiphany.

GEORGE
Pagans.

With enormous relief, Albus embraces
his daughter.

Blasius falls to his knees and prays to
avert a possible retribution.

Sabra pushes her father away.

SABRA
Did you see what he did?!

ALBUS
Of course I saw--

SABRA
He...he...interfered!

GEORGE
Intervened.

SABRA
Interfered!

GEORGE
And how do expect your...your goddess
to vindicate this--?

SABRA
What world do you live in? Do you not
know about--

George pushes out his neck and widens
his eyes to coax an answer to his
specific question.

SABRA
Drought!

GEORGE
She'll punish you with drought?

SABRA
Amongst a host other ills!

GEORGE
Juturna punishes you with drought
because you don't give her pet
alligator three square meals a day?

Albus wants to shake George's hands
but not sure it wise in front of his
daughter, smiles at him instead.

SABRA
It's a dragon!

Sabra puts her hands over her ears
and prays. George is in her face
nonetheless.

GEORGE
I know what it is your highness. And
now that I have rescued you, what
other piece of havoc will she wreak?
Rain perhaps? Drought is obviously not
working, thanks to me.

SABRA
Your disrespect...is repugnant!

Sabra turns to her father.

SABRA
Arrest him.

GEORGE/ALBUS
What?!

SABRA
Arrest him.

ALBUS
Why? On what charge?

Blasius recalibrates opportunistically.

BLASIUS
This man has shown contempt for our
customs and blasphemed Juturna's
divinity.

GEORGE
You would think a goddess can fight her
own battles.

Sabra kicks George full in the crown
jewels. He drops to his knees. Blasius
echoes.

BLASIUS
Arrest this man!

Albus hisses at the priest.

ALBUS
Let me guess, Juturna wills it?

BLASIUS
No.

Albus notices a crowd of villagers
gathered behind Blasius. A few mean and
large men.

BLASIUS
The people will it.

Crlank!

EXT. CASTLE - DAY

A shabby, modest castle blights the
hilly landscape.

INT. JAIL CELL

Albus stands inside the dark dingy stone
room. The iron door open behind him.

George sits on the stone floor with his
head against the wall. His eyes are
closed as he speaks.

GEORGE
Who are you?

ALBUS
Albus.

GEORGE
Your castle?

ALBUS
My castle.

Albus turns to close the door behind
him and squats down to George's eye-
level.

ALBUS
I will give you half of everything I
own.

George opens his eyes. Frowns. Albus
whispers.

ALBUS
If you slay the creature.

George chortles as he stands. Moves to
the barred window and peers outside.

GEORGE
You think I can slay your Dragon?

ALBUS
You are a soldier.

George's smile vanishes.

GEORGE
Was.

George sees Ashkelon wandering down
below outside the castle walls and
whispers a passage he heard somewhere
to himself.

GEORGE
"The Dragon stood on the shore of the
sea..."

Louder.

GEORGE
The Beast is not your problem.

Albus snaps.

ALBUS
I know this!

Calms his frustration.

ALBUS
I know this.

Who are you?

GEORGE
That... is not important.

EXT. LAKE OF SILENE - FLASHBACK BEGINS

From Albus's point of view he sees
George making the sign of the cross by
touching his forehead, chest and each
shoulder whilst the Dragon scurries
back into the water.

ALBUS (O.S.)
You are a follower.

FLASHBACK ENDS

INT. JAIL CELL - CONTINUOUS

ALBUS
A disciple...

George frowns perturbedly.

ALBUS
...of the man who returned from the
dead, a god in flesh, destroyer of all
other gods.

George turns to face Albus with
suspicious curiosity.

GEORGE
Who are you?

Albus smiles.

ALBUS
That...is not important. What is
important, is your price.

GEORGE
Listen. King. I'm not the man you think
I am.

George surrenders back down on the floor.

ALBUS
Nor am I. But what I know is that every
man has a price.

Albus softens his plea.

ALBUS
Save us from this hex.

EXT. JAIL CELL - CONTINUOUS

Sabra stands outside the door -
listening.

INT. JAIL CELL - CONTINUOUS

George closes his eyes.

EXT. NICOMEDIA - DAY - FLASHBACK BEGINS

A formidable city sprawls over the
horizon.

TITLE CARD: Imperial city of Nicomedia.
Part of the Roman Empire.

INT. SENATE - CONTINUOUS

An indoor Roman-style amphitheater
occupied by men donned in traditional
white robes. The hall swarms with
the buzz of murmuring politicians -
something controversial's afoot.

On the front stage, the center of
attention, sits the four rulers
characterized by the wreaths on each of
their heads.

DIOCLETIAN, MAXIMIAN, CONSTANTIUS &
GERALIUS - Only two of these men are
important.

DIOCLETIAN 60s, the wise agitated
eldest.

Beside him rises the younger, bulkier
and meaner GERALIUS 40s. Geralius
simply raises his arms and the room
falls silent.

There is a fierce scar underneath
Geralius's left eye. He paces the hall
with magniloquence.

GERALIUS
Are we not Rome? Are we not an Empire?
Are we not made of Iron?

Soldiers, Centurions, Tribunes, Caesars
we are, but Iron, an Empire - we are
not.

Not quite.

He stops to look at his audience.

GERALIUS
Some of us have pledged our allegiance
to the standard, our legions, our
Caesars and our gods. Some of us. Yes.

But others...

...have moved the boundary stone of our
forefathers.

Geralius continues walking - past the
Tribunes equally spaced along the outer
wall.

GERALIUS
...they no longer follow our customs,
they no longer follow the gods of our
fathers - but a man!

A man claiming not only to have come
from the gods, but to be a god himself?

Again Geralius stops. This time right
next to a particular Tribune...

GERALIUS
I know this, for I have seen them...

...A well-groomed soldier, a younger -

GEORGE

Geralius sneers.

GERALIUS
...and I am vexed.

George stoic and immovable, even though
he knows he's being addressed.

Geralius walks up to one of the many
plinths boasting some or other piece of
ceramic ornament.

GERALIUS
Vexed for we do not have their all. And
if we do not have their all...

Geralius stops beside one such plinth
displaying a ceramic vase.

GERALIUS
...then our Empire becomes...

Geralius gently puts his palm against
the vase and pushes it off the plinth.

GERALIUS
 ...brittle.

The vase smashes on the ground.

GERALIUS
Rumors of men masquerading as the 'one'
god, and what is a rumor, but clay my
friends?

Empires of Iron, are not mixed with
clay. For if they were...

Geralius looks down at the powder and
broken pieces at his feet.

Diocletian is visibly angry. He squirms
in his chair. A politician suddenly
shouts from the audience.

MAN
What do you propose?

Geralius walks slowly towards a plinth
with a wooden ballot box on top of it.

GERALIUS
A gentle push. A benevolent nudge.

Geralius stops behind the ballot-box
and takes off his wreath. Looks at it.

GERALIUS
We as rulers have a responsibility to
our soldiers, like fathers would have
towards their sons.

Geralius puts the wreath back on his
head and looks down at the scroll and
quill lying on top of the ballot-box.

GERALIUS
One week.

One week to allow them to renew
their sacrifices to the gods of their
fathers, and...

...to begin again.

Geralius signs the edict.

Like a sudden storm his demeanor grows
menacing. He drops the scroll into the
box.

GERALIUS
And so we mend our Empire. As iron
would sharpen iron.

Senators clamber down the stairs to
vote.

Geralius smiles smugly as he watches
Diocletian, visibly irritated, rush
from the room.

EXT. A QUIET CORRIDOR - LATER

Diocletian and George stand whispering
with some secrecy and urgency.

GEORGE
This is nothing but a persecution!

DIOCLETIAN
Is there somewhere you can go? A
property you need to sell?

GEORGE
You would have me run from this?

DIOCLETIAN
Why do you surrender to this man?! It
is a Palestinian faith--

GEORGE
We've been over this.

DIOCLETIAN
Whatever your belief, I promised your
father I would do all I can to keep you
from harm.

GEORGE
I'm too young to retire Diocletian.

Diocletian puts his hand on George's
arm and speaks tenderly like a loving
father would to a son.

DIOCLETIAN
George listen to me. We sometimes win,
by losing.

George pleads.

GEORGE
But this is my home!

DIOCLETIAN
Think it through.

Diocletian removes his hand from
George's arm and straightens himself.

DIOCLETIAN
And now, as your emperor, I urge you to
reconsider. If you do not leave, I will
have but one choice, to discharge you.

Both men look at each other, both
visibly perturbed.

EXT. COURTYARD - NIGHT

George walks briskly out of his house
and drops a number of satchels on a
wooden cart tied behind Ashkelon.

GERALIUS (O.S.)
I always knew you were a deserter.

George swings around to meet Geralius
emerging from the shadows with a couple
of Roman soldiers.

GERALIUS
Abandoned your parents to their demise.

George hisses.

GEORGE
I was fourteen.

GERALIUS
Oh, that's right. Not yet a man.

Geralius steps up to George and taps
him across the face with a few leather
straps he has in his hands. Turns
his head curiously as George doesn't
respond.

GERALIUS
How novel is this new truth - Turning
the other cheek?

Geralius hits him again but harder.

GERALIUS
This is actually quite fun.

The soldiers laugh.

GERALIUS
We shall introduce this to the
Colosseum, I think.

He makes another attempt but George
seizes his wrist.

A Soldier steps forward and puts a knife
on George's throat. George remains
fearless.

GEORGE
I'm flattered you would go to all this
trouble to draw up an edict just for
me.

Geralius pulls out the iron cross from
inside George's shirt.

GERALIUS
And yet, you will not stay? You will
not fight for your faith?

Geralius looks down and sees George's
knuckles white around on sword.

GERALIUS
Go on...

He looks back and sneers at George,
running his forefinger along the scar
under his own eye.

GERALIUS
...why not finish your father's legacy?

George removes his hand off his sword.

GEORGE
This is a new world Geralius. You can
no longer enforce anything. Your iron,
is sinking.

A few soldiers drag in the body of a
dead man, NIKOLAS, and drops it at the
feet of George. George recognizes him.

FLASHBACK BEGINS: George pushes Nikolas
underneath the water. Brings him back
up. Nikolas, bewildered, runs.

FLASHBACK ENDS.

GERALIUS
And yet you force forgiveness of sins
through this strange water ritual on
the unsuspecting.

How are we different?

George hisses.

GEORGE
Do I not have a week to think on this?
Pushes the soldier, with the knife at
his throat, away.

Geralius stands closer and hisses.

GERALIUS
In one week, If you can convert an
entire village to this new religion
of yours, within the confines of our
Empire, I shall reconsider the edict.

Geralius turns away.

GERALIUS
And of course, do not forget the
sign...this... Baptismal bath.

In fact, I am overcome with benevolence
I shall assist you in this new found
discipleship.

Soldiers suddenly grab George and pin
him to the cart.

Geralius draws his knife and lunges on
George to carve a bloody cross into his
neck.

George growls getting one arm free
punches the nearest soldier and by
retracting his elbow, smashes it into
the nose of the opposite soldier,
then head-butts Geralius, cutting the
opposite cheek where his father had
left his scar.

Geralius falls back as George jumps
onto Ashkelon, circles before kicking
his horse towards the exits.

More soldiers pour from the shadows
with horses, ready to pursue. Geralius
touches his cheek and looks at the
blood on his fingers. Sneers at the
fleeing George.

GERALIUS
Have your week.

George vanishes into the night.

FLASHBACK ENDS.

We see George's face underneath the
water. His eyes calm. The cross carved
into the side of his neck. He suddenly
pulls out his head from the water.

EXT. CASTLE - DAY

George turns away from the well in the
center courtyard of the castle. He
faces Albus, drying his face.

ALBUS
Just to be clear...

Albus steps closer and whispers.

ALBUS
...you want the entire village of
Silene... baptized!?

He looks around making certain no-one
is overhearing.

ALBUS
And you will slay the Dragon?

SABRA (O.S.)
You're letting him go?!

Like a boulder running down a hill,
Sabra approaches.

SABRA
What of his punishment?

ALBUS
We, he, has agreed on his penance.

Sabra folds her arms.

SABRA
And?

ALBUS
Sabra. I know you think Juturna is
unhappy with us that she sent the
Dragon to plague us, to what end no one
knows.

But I think different.

SABRA
Different how?

She sees George pulling his spear from
the scabbard in Ashkelon's saddle and
begins sharpening it. Realizing what
was about to transpose Sabra begins to
laugh.

SABRA
He's not...

Growls.

SABRA
He's not!?

Aargh! And I suppose he's taking half
of all we own for it. Father you cannot
do this? Blasius will be so, so, so...

ALBUS
Blasius is not your father! He answers
to me!

GEORGE (O.S.)
You answer to me!

Albus and Sabra both turn to face George
in the middle of reprimanding Ashkelon.

GEORGE
You got that? You're not a cow, you
can't go off grazing when you feel like
it.

George cuts off a small tuft of
Ashkelon's mane and shows him. Ashkelon
turns away, not wanting to look.

GEORGE
Am I playing now huh? I mean what I say
horse!

Whilst Ashkelon whimpers George suddenly
becomes aware of Albus and Sabra's eyes
on him.

GEORGE
Is this your castle?

SABRA
He has poisoned us Father--

ALBUS
Enough!

Albus answers George.

ALBUS
This is my castle.

GEORGE
Then that's my price.

Albus pauses before giving one simple
single nod in agreement.

EXT. LAKE OF SILENE - DAY

George stands looking out across the
lake. Spear in one hand and sword in
the other he paces impatiently.

GEORGE
Little bitty ol' lizard. That's what's
doing Georgie. No more running.

He hears something behind him and turns
to see

SABRA

A short distance away, spreading what
looks like a picnic blanket. She sits
down with a basket of food and starts
eating.

He thrusts his spear into the sand and
walks up to her. Looks down at the food
and bends down to help himself. Quickly
she moves the food away. He frowns.
Goes again but this time she cracks him
right in the jaw with a bottle.

He's angry.

GEORGE
You should thank me!

Rubs his jaw.

SABRA
You're not so good at waiting are you?

Snaps.

GEORGE
I am good...at waiting.
Unconvinced.

SABRA
What's your plan oh glorious knight of
the realm?

George storms back to the edge of the
lake. Paces. Thinks. Picks up a stone
and throws it far in to the lake.
Another.

Picks up a smaller pebble and this time
bounces it along the water's surface.

It skips four times before sinking.
George is pleased with himself.

Turns to smile at a dead-pan Sabra. His
smile vanishes.

He suddenly touches his shoulder.
Rotates it to warm it up.

He slowly walks back to her.

GEORGE
Why not just starve him?

SABRA
Because if we don't feed him, he makes
his way...

She glances up towards the village. He
follows her eyes as they return to the
piece of fruit in her hand.

SABRA
Once was enough.

Quickly she stands, making ready to
leave.

Bending over to help her with the
blanket his cross slips out from his
tunic. Sabra notices and stops.

SABRA
You're a zealot.

George quickly puts away his cross.

GEORGE
And you're harlot.

Sabra punches him full in the jaw,
second in the solar plexus and a third
kick to the crotch.

George drops to his knees. He grunts
barely audible.

GEORGE
Stop...with...the...violence.

Falls over. Rolls on his back to catch
his breath.

GEORGE
It's true then.

Sabra grabs her picnic basket while
George groans.

GEORGE
Your priest is a bad, bad man.

SABRA
You know nothing about Blasius!

GEORGE
I know enough.

George stands with difficulty.

GEORGE
Who in their right mind would willingly
go to their death?

She throws her half-eaten piece of
fruit at him.

SABRA
You follow a man who has done just
that! That makes you a hypocrite, sir!

She storms off. He shouts after her.

GEORGE
Ah, so we're at the 'my-god-will-beat-
up-our-god' phase in our relationship!

George, equally as angry, strides
towards his spear, and grabbing it,
aims it Sabra's back.

Pauses... growls... turns away...
then...

...with an almighty chuck, throws his
spear towards the trees.

Snarls as he grabs his shoulder,
looking very much like an aggravated
old injury.

The spear whistles through the air and
disappears in the trees.

EXT. ROAD - MINUTES LATER

George stands in the middle of the road
that leads around the top of the beach.

He looks right and sees the faint trails
of smoke from the village.

He looks left and sees the cliff that protrudes out over the lake.

He looks up and sees his

SPEAR

stuck at the very top of the tree.

Picking up a rock he throws it upwards... misses... it falls straight back down and George has to step out the way to miss it.

Again he throws.

This time the rock falls and hits Ashkelon's saddle whose appeared from nowhere.

George looks at his horse who is also looking up into the trees.

Sneers before looking down at his sword lying on the ground.

GEORGE
I don't have time for this.

Picks it up and sheaths it. Then looks out over the lake below.

GEORGE
So you're hungry.

George turns to face Ashkelon like he's suddenly got an idea.

GEORGE
The Dragon's hungry.

Cut to...

EXT. LAKE OF SILENE - MINUTES LATER

Ashkelon is tied to the stake, oblivious
at first that he is bait.

He smells the ground, the faint blood
stains on the sand.

His ears suddenly prick up. He steps
backwards and pulls at his reins.

George stands sword drawn. Clumsily
twirling it like some inept apprentice.
Drops it. Looks at his hand and fingers
and frowns. Opens and closes them to
see if it is still working. Looks at
the trees where his spear is resting on
some branches.

Picks up his sword and talks to it.

GEORGE
You... need to lose some weight.

He sees Ashkelon chewing on his rein.

GEORGE
Horse! Cut it out! I need you to stand
there and look pretty. Shouldn't be
hard for a high-hat.

Ashkelon protests with a whinny.

GEORGE
Don't worry, I'm not going to let him
get to you...

Much.

George stands ankle-deep facing the
water. Legs apart and stabbing the air.
Shouts in frustration.

GEORGE
Come on!

A series of montage shots.

-- George sitting on the beach.

-- George skipping stones.

-- George practicing his sword skills.
Getting better. More confident.

-- George sheaths and unsheathes his
sword at greater speed, like some
gunslinger.

-- Practices throwing his sword at a
tree. The handle hits bark a couple
of times, until he finally gets the
blade end to stick. His arms go up
triumphantly.

GEORGE
I should join the circus.

He then points at the trees his spear
is tangled in.

GEORGE
Don't need you anymore.

-- Sits against the stake, sleeping.
Suddenly wakes up with a jolt, grabbing
his sword he almost stabs Ashkelon.

-- George stands on the beach with the
sword resting across his shoulders. The
sun low in the sky.
George finally turns to Ashkelon.

GEORGE
Your lucky day Ash. I guess he doesn't
like horse.

She.

Unties Ashkelon's reins from the stake.

GEORGE
Get us some wood will ya?

George pulls out his cross and looks at
it.

GEORGE
Maybe we scared her away.

EXT. VILLAGE OF SILENE - DAY

The village bustles with activity. The
trails of smoke trickle up into the
air.

Ashkelon ambles into the town square,
carrying George in the saddle.

Stops.

George scans his surroundings. Villagers
reciprocate with suspicion.

He fixes his eyes on the temple of
Juturna, twisting his expression more
menacing.

GEORGE
There's the boss.

His eyes shift and quickly fixes on a
shop front. A neatly painted sign of
a 'scroll with wings', hangs from two
chains.

Sabra stands out the front. Peering at
him with arms folded.

George leans forward whispers to
Ashkelon.

GEORGE
Silene's herald. No wonder she plays by
the rules.

He coaxes Ashkelon towards her.
Clippity-clop he stops in front of her.
Gets off his horse and gives her a half-
hearted flourish with his arm by way of
greeting.

GEORGE
You father owns this village.

She snaps coldly.

SABRA
And therefore his daughter shouldn't
work.

Shrugs it off.

GEORGE
What did you feed him before?

Before you spoilt it by feeding it
handsome young maidens--

Sabra frowns. So does George.

GEORGE
Feeding it maid--

SABRA
Sheep.

George opens his mouth but Sabra
interrupts him.

SABRA
We've run out--

GEORGE
Cows?--

SABRA
Before sheep--

TARQUIN (O.S.)
And goats before cows.

A mean burly giant of a man, TARQUIN
40s, growing a bush for a beard, takes
Sabra's side. Wiping his bloody hands
on his apron.

Either side of Tarquin, in stark
contrast, slips in two clean shaven
zombie-looking BEEFHEADS menacingly
eying George.

George chuckles.

GEORGE
So you're all vegetarians then--

SABRA
Chickens.

Tarquin holds up his bloody fingers for
George to see and grunts.

TARQUIN
So you're the Dragon slayer?

His two burly Beefhead friends spin
their own quirky brand of laughter.

GEORGE
I think you'd pass as a cow.

Tarquin immediately stops laughing.

George leans forward and holds up a
coin.

GEORGE
How about it?

George nods towards the two.

GEORGE
Bring the sheep along.

Sabra prevents Tarquin from lunging at
George. A shake of her head gets him to
back down.

SABRA
Allow our visitor to concentrate his
full efforts on the Dragon.

Tarquin smiles, points at George as if
to say "I'll get you later". Beefhead
One spits on the ground in front of
George.

George looks down and drops the coin
right in the pile of spit.

GEORGE
I'll take one of your chickens.

EXT. LAKE - DAY

The chicken is tied to the stake. A
little perturbed as it flutters around
trying to get away. PWAK-PUK-PUK!

George stands nearby and smiles. Looks
at Ashkelon standing some distance away
and points to the chicken.

GEORGE
This is how you make a noise Ash. Learn
from an expert.

Ashkelon lifts his nose in a disdainful snort before strutting himself into the bush.

GEORGE
Snob.

Shouts after him in thick sarcasm.

GEORGE
While you're up there do me the courtesy of getting my spear milord!

Adds under his breath.

GEORGE
Ectomorph.

George mimics the chicken as if trying to irritate his horse.

GEORGE
Pwak-puk-puk-pkah!

Turns to the lake. Touches his cross under his shirt and draws his sword. Does the chicken war-cry even louder.

GEORGE
Pwak-puk-puk-pkah!

In the bush, behind a tree, Sabra stands spying at George. Her frown turns to fascination. Her fascination leaks onto her face in the form of the faintest of smiles. Her beautiful black locks sway like the curtain to a brothel as she moves out from behind the tree when suddenly...

George stops his chicken impersonation and quickly turns around, looking straight at Sabra.

Taken completely by surprise, she instinctively ducks back in behind the tree and bites her lip for being caught.

George throws up his arms as if to say, "I've seen you woman."

Sabra pushes herself out from behind the tree to face him, making a show of her confidence.

GEORGE
Pwak-puk-puk.

Sabra turns around and walks briskly back to her village.

George smiles as he turns to once again face the lake.

His eyes widen as he sees the Dragon's black eyes resting just above the waterline.

He grips his sword tighter and bares his own clenched teeth.

GEORGE
Still time Georgie.

As if a tsunami's about to erupt the Dragon quivers underneath the water, sending out battalions of ripples.

George squints his eyes to mimics the Dragon.

The chicken pwak-pwaks behind him. He
points his sword at the chicken.

GEORGE
That's right. Tastes like chicken.

The Dragon slowly lowers his head back
into the water and vanishes.

George grips his sword with both hands.
Takes out his cross and bends his knees.

Nothing.

Serenity descends on the lake...for
now.

George eventually lowers his sword.

GEORGE
If that's what you want...handsome
young maidens it is.

EXT. SILENE - DAY

George stands in the village square.

His eyes narrow while he slowly turns
to take in all that is around him. As
if he's looking for something.

Like some tourist he too is being
casually and suspiciously observed by
the villagers.

In front of the Temple of Juturna stands
Blasius. Arms folded and fuming.

Albus smugly takes his side.

ALBUS
Blasius.

Blasius wrenches the words from his own
mouth.

BLASIUS
My Lord.

ALBUS
I like him.

BLASIUS
Juturna is not mocked.

Blasius and Albus watch some of the
villagers in the process of boarding up
their windows.

BLASIUS
It's only a matter of time.

Albus winces.

ALBUS
We all get hungry Blasius.

Walks away.

George watches Albus walking away from
Blasius.

His eyes shift to

CHARLOTTE 20s

A young voluptuous beauty trying her best to inconspicuously make her way towards Blasius. Her bosom bouncing precariously near her low-cut frock.

She smiles at Blasius but with a quick shake of his head she halts in her tracks and turns on her heels.

Blasius turns and storms back inside the temple.

George smiles like he's found his prey.

He storms her.

GEORGE
How much?

Charlotte the harlot feigns shock. Looks around.

CHARLOTTE
I am not--

GEORGE
How much?

Charlotte surrenders and holds up three fingers.

George grabs her hand and makes for the lake. She giggles at the rough treatment, oblivious that she's about to be sacrificed.
Standing at the doorway of her post-office, Sabra's eyes burn as she watches George and Charlotte disappear into the woods.

A villager approaches Sabra but quickly she closes the door and turns over the CLOSED sign. Follows.

Unsure turns back to face her store. Throws up her hands in surrender. Turns and follow.

EXT. LAKE - DAY

Charlotte and George reach the beach.

Charlotte, still smiling, suddenly sees the sacrificial stake in front of them. Her smile vanishes in an instant and she stops dead in her tracks. Her hands slips from George's grip.

He turns to face her and sees her sudden anguish.

Charlotte's eyes widen. He finger waves.

CHARLOTTE
I'm not going to be your...your...

She slowly retreats as George clumsily tries to put her at ease.

GEORGE
I'm not going to let anything happen to you. I just need a lure.

Charlotte turns to run but George catches her in a few short strides and like a sack of potatoes hurls her over his shoulder.

CHARLOTTE
No! No!

She kicks and protests as George carries
her towards the stake.

Drops her back on her feet.

CHARLOTTE
I protest! I protest!

He smiles at her.

CHARLOTTE
What?

GEORGE
I didn't think people still talked that
way.

She bangs her fists onto his face.

He steps back. With fists flaying, she
follows, but is yanked back by the

ROPE

already tied around her waist.

George tosses her three coins.

Charlotte's eyes widen even further as
she fumbles with the indomitable knot.

CHARLOTTE
You can't do this!

George draws his sword and faces the
lake.

86

GEORGE
He has to come through me first, wench.

Charlotte abandons the knot and runs
around the stake screaming.

CHARLOTTE
Help! Help! Someone help me!

George straightens himself and grins.

GEORGE
That's good. Nice and loud.

Charlotte runs in a few circles around
the stake, unaware that her rope is
growing shorter, until she finally bangs
herself into it and falls backwards
onto her buttocks.

Surrenders and lies down.

Her sobbing makes George's grin vanish.

As he steps forward he sees someone
rushing him from his peripheral. Too
late he's tackled hard and falls to the
sand with Tarquin on top of him.

Tarquin quickly stands and pulls George
up with him, then punches him full in
the jaw.

As George hits the sand Charlotte
springs upright and smiles through her
tears.

CHARLOTTE
T-T!

87

Quickly George gets to his feet but
before he can get his fists up, Beefhead
One and Beefhead Two flank him, each
grabbing one of his arms.

GEORGE
Nothing like a fair fight.

Like a canon Tarquin's fist is about to
roar when...
George pulls Beefhead One towards him...

Tarquin's fist connects Beefhead One
right in the solar plexus. He rocks
back with an almighty wheeze.

In the process George lands on top of
Beefhead Two and quickly gives him a
good old-fashioned backwards head-butt.

Rolls off just as Tarquin makes a grab
for him.

George hops to his feet and the two men
momentarily square each other. Tarquin
the first to swing but Beefhead Two pulls
at George's ankles and topples him over
just as Tarquin's punch whooshes the
air above George's head.

Tarquin picks up George's sword and
putting his boot on George's chest,
lifts the sword for a fatal blow.

Hisses.

TARQUIN
She is my woman!

SABRA (O.S.)
Tarquin!

Approaching she holds out her hand for
the sword. Tarquin smiles as he gladly
hands it to her and steps off George.
Expecting Sabra to finish him off--

SABRA
Leave him.

Tarquin's grin hits the ground. Sabra
makes her way to Charlotte with the
sword.

Beefhead One wants to storm George but
Tarquin, with open jaw holds out his
arm preventing him.

George quickly crawls backwards away
from the three men holding his own
bloodied face.

All four men watch Sabra free Charlotte
from her ropes.

The buxom runs towards Tarquin but with
a nod of his head, she ninety degrees
scurries off to the village.

Sabra throws down George's sword on
the sand in front of him and repeats
herself to a stunned Tarquin.

SABRA
Leave him. Let us see him fare.

Tarquin, uncertain whether to wince or to cry, turns and storms off with his consorts.

George stands to meet her animosity.

SABRA
All you had to do was ask.

Behind them the sun barely clings to the horizon.

Sabra walks away, shouting as she does.

SABRA
Tomorrow!

Leaving George in some sort of emotional limbo.

EXT. LAKE SILENE - DAY

Sabra stands in her long white dress and wreath in front of the sacrificial stake, like she did when her and George had first met.

She appears to be alone on the sand. George nowhere to be seen.

Sabra looks out over the lake, raises her arms up either side of herself and closes her eyes.

GEORGE (O.S.)
Why do you do that?

Sabra opens her eyes.

GEORGE
Why do you close your eyes?

She looks at the sky as if being asked
to endure a chore.

George is lying at her feet, buried
beneath the sand.
His face, and his sword lying on his
chest, is barely visible. She snaps.

SABRA
Do you not know these sacrificial
moments before Juturna are to be
endured with solemnity?

Again she closes her eyes.

GEORGE
Your paganism was once my paganism.

Sabra bites her lip and tries to keep
her eyes closed.

GEORGE
You used the word 'endured'.

Again she snaps.

SABRA
And?!

GEORGE
Well, it's like admitting that your
paganism is in fact a tradition. A
duty. And somewhat of a foul one I'll
add.

Her voice a little louder. Her arms a
little shakier.

SABRA
And what of your rituals? Here, take
a bath, and all your wrongs are simply
forgotten.

George pushes his entire head out of
the sand to take a look at her.

SABRA
Yes. I know your paganism too.

GEORGE
Baptism is symbolic.

Sabra stands closer and puts her foot
on his forehead pushing his head back
in the ground.

SABRA
You mean simplistic.

GEORGE
Simplistic?!

George pushes away her foot and pulls
himself out of the ground like a zombie,
sand pouring from every part of him.

GEORGE
Do you not regret anything?!

SABRA
Oh I can think of one thing.

GEORGE
Let me make this clear. Your goddess
Juturna, does not exist.

SABRA
Step away.

George steps closer.

GEORGE
Or what? Juturna's curse? A cloud will
fall on my head?

SABRA
Just because we don't see the gods does
not mean they are not manifested.

GEORGE
The God of Heaven's been seen.

SABRA
Do you believe every rumor?

GEORGE
Your worth, your weight is proportional
to what you worship.

SABRA
What does that mean?

He's in her face.

GEORGE
If you're going to worship air. Then
you yourself...air.

Sabra turns and storms off. George shouts
after her.

GEORGE
There you go again, running when you
should be staying, and staying when you
should be running.

George frowns at his own words.

Continues to shout after her.

GEORGE
A father having to give up his daughter
on some figment, is not right!

She stops. Turns and walks back towards
him.

Behind them in the water, The Dragon
watches. His eyeballs move from George
to Sabra as the dialogue flows.

SABRA
But a father giving up his son is...
right?

Isn't that how your story goes? In
fact, I'm pretty sure that if I
was a son, this sacrifice would be
acceptable?

She steps towards him and hisses.

SABRA
It is because I am a woman.

GEORGE
What?! This has nothing to do--

SABRA
And now, you'll probably follow in the
tradition of the caveman to put me back
in my place.

GEORGE
That is... unacceptable woman!

They eyeball each other like two
warriors before...

SABRA
Woman? I rest.

George, in a sudden frenzy, attacks
the stake with his sword, carving and
slicing as if he were fighting a horde
of zombies.

Sabra, however, sees the Dragon rise
quietly out of the water. She swallows,
straightens herself and walks towards
him.

George's sword gets stuck in the stake.
He pulls. Stuck.

Looking over his shoulder he sees Sabra
moving towards the Dragon. George
mumbles.

GEORGE
Rotten timing Georgie!

He pulls again and this time frees his
sword and hurls it at the Dragon.

The sword pierces its ear, going right
through it. The Dragon shrills as blood
spurts.

The Dragon drops forward onto the sand
and immediately slithers towards him.
His tail knocks Sabra over and into the
water.

George whips out his cross, grips it tight in his hand and holds it up as the Dragon pounces.

The earth shakes as the Dragon slams down right in front of George with an unearthly shrill, its teeth an inch away from the cross.

We see, just for a split second, an invisible magnetic field, that surrounds the cross.

The gone, but enough to repel the Dragon once more as she turns and flees back to her watery cave.

Sabra's crawls out of the water and out of breath.

George stands looking at his cross and whispers.

GEORGE
Still works.

Puts it back inside his tunic as Sabra, drenched, steps towards him. Together they stare at the lake - somewhat stupefied.

SABRA
Why is she scared of you?

GEORGE
I've been meaning to ask, how do you know its a she?

She looks at him.

SABRA
You were holding something. What was
it?

GEORGE
Perhaps she knows.

SABRA
Knows what?

George picks up his sword.

GEORGE
Juturna knows that I am to be her
assassin.

Sabra puts her hands over her ears,
shocked that her goddess is being
diminished albeit through words.

GEORGE
If she won't come out...

The lake quiet.

GEORGE
I'm going to need a boat.

EXT. NICOMEDIA - DAY

From a distance Nicomedia rises like
the Babel of old. A city street bustles
with activity outside a government
building.

INT. GERALIUS'S OFFICES - CONTINUOUS

Geralius sits behind an over-sized
table pouring over some documents and
scrolls.

A knock. A soldier enters. Salutes,
then steps aside to let in

GNAEUS
The fat man enters.

The soldier waits for Geralius, who
doesn't acknowledge either of the men.
The soldier remains in the room and
closes the door.

Puts his hand on his sword as Gnaeus
walks towards Geralius's desk.

Geralius still doesn't look up. Gnaeus
uncertain whether to bow, courtesy or
salute. Speaks instead.

GNAEUS
I hear...there is a reward.

Geralius still doesn't acknowledge
Gnaeus.

GNAEUS
A soldier.

Deserter.

Geralius puts down the document he is
reading and looks up straight at Gnaeus.

Gnaeus strokes his beard like he's
waiting for something.

Geralius moves the bag of coins, already
on his desk, closer to Gnaeus.

Gnaeus immediately snatches it and
buries it somewhere in his tunic.

GNAEUS
I followed him to Silene.

Geralius's eyes pierce the fat man for
his betrayal nonetheless.

The soldier's sword unsheathes, behind
him.

EXT. SILENE - DAY

The sun rises over the village.

From the village square runs the main
street.

The tavern, sign posted, halfway up the
main street.

A narrower street to the right of it.

In the alley lies

GEORGE.

Flat on his back in the mud. Empty
wineskin on his chest.

Ashkelon struts towards him and wiggles his slobbery lips over George's face. George shakes as he wakes. Disgruntled, pushes his horse away.

Sits upright and immediately blenches from his head pain and his swollen left eye.

He sees Sabra standing at the entrance to the alley, stone-faced.

SABRA
'Anything he wants' he says. You've turned my own father against me.

George backs himself up against the wall of the tavern. Touches his head.

SABRA
Why are you running?

He tries to look at her through the early morning glare.

GEORGE
I am not running.

SABRA
They say you are a deserter.

GEORGE
I have a farm. Somewhere.

Now, I am lost.

He stumbles to his feet.

SABRA
What happens if you fail?

GEORGE
I don't go home.

Sabra frowns, almost sympathetically.
Turns on her heels and leaves him.

EXT. LAKE - DAY

A small rowboat bobs in the water in
the center of the lake.

In the boat lies rope and some large
stones.

George ties one end of the rope to one
of the benches inside the boat.

He looks at Sabra, also in the boat

GEORGE
I can do this on my own.

Sabra looks out towards the shore.

We see about twenty villagers,
spectating, making themselves
comfortable with picnic blankets and
baskets.

SABRA
This is too good to miss.

Her language is less confrontational.

SABRA
I am still my father's daughter and so,
front row seat for me.

GEORGE
So, a circus.

Sabra gleeful.

SABRA
Oh it is even better than the circus.

She looks down into the water.

SABRA
Jump in and take a stab? That's your
plan?

GEORGE
Too simplistic for you?

George ties the other end to himself.

GEORGE
Why do you not fear, for yourself?

SABRA
I have a duty to my people.

GEORGE
So, as a habit, you always push your
own desires aside?

SABRA
Paganism is not as selfish as you had
thought?

She smiles. He replies.

GEORGE
You do not fear, because you do not
love.

SABRA
That makes two of us then?

George takes the smallest stone and
begins sharpening his sword.

GEORGE
How old were you?

Sabra looks at him and frowns.

GEORGE
When you lost her?
She looks away.

SABRA
Ten.

GEORGE
And Juturna took her place.

George checks the sharpness of his
sword.

Sabra leans over the edge of the boat
and runs her fingers through the water.

SABRA
Why this...water dipping?

GEORGE
It's called baptism.

He pauses to judge the sincerity of her
question. Satisfied, he proceeds.

GEORGE
The man I follow--

SABRA
Jesu?

GEORGE
Jesu.

Taught that our wrongs are forgotten
when they are buried in the water.

We can begin again.

SABRA
Begin again? Why begin again?

GEORGE
You never wanted to start again? A
clean scroll?

Sabra doesn't understand.

SABRA
A clean scroll? Why?

George sits down. Holds out his hand
inviting her to shake it.

GEORGE
George.

Confused, she looks at his hand..

SABRA
I know who you are.

GEORGE
A bit presumptuous don't you think?

SABRA
I don't--

GEORGE
We just met?

He repeats the gesture.

GEORGE
George.

She gets the game.

SABRA
What are you doing here?

GEORGE
I've come to slay your dragon.

Sabra looks out over the lake and
around her.

SABRA
What dragon?

George clenches his teeth. This is
going to be hard.

GEORGE
What are you doing in a boat with a
strange man?

She suddenly becomes overtly theatrical.

SABRA
Wait... did you say dragon!?

Sabra suddenly stands. She shakes her
body with fake fear. The boat rocks as
she climbs on her seat plank.

SABRA
Oh, I think I might faint!

GEORGE
Alright!

George is visibly irritated. While
she sits back down smiling, he stands
grumpily and picks up a rock. With Stone
in one hand and sword in the other he
puts his foot on the edge of the boat
readying himself to jump.

Sabra nods towards the villagers
increasing in numbers on the shore.

SABRA
You know Silenes will not agree to
this... Baptism.

GEORGE
He told you?

SABRA
The world cannot be changed all at
once.

GEORGE
They will do as your father says if
they are to remain on his land.

SABRA
It would be easier to plant a hoof and
grow a cow.

George looks out over the villagers.
Thinking.

She smirks like she knows she's right.

SABRA
You cannot even see how forcing this
upon us, is empty of any kind of
sincerity?

George looks down at the water.
Thinking.

Sees a glimpse of a shadow move
underneath.

Sabra notices his lingering pause.

George throws the rock in the water,
not jumping in after it.

She frowns at his strange strategy.

GEORGE
Then I won't be slaying your dragon.

Smug.

SABRA
Father will be disappointed.

George sits down in front of her and
looks straight at her.

GEORGE
I'm going to catch Juturna's Dragon.
You will be baptized. Every last one
of you. Then only, will I slay your
dragon.

The hardness instantaneously returns to
Sabra's face.

EXT/INT. SILENE'S TAVERN - NIGHT

Raucous laughter.

George walks into the room like some
gunslinger new in town. The roof
extraordinarily low.

The place falls silent, you can hear a
rat carrying off with floor treasure.

George walks up to the bar, past Tarquin
the butcher.

The place returns to a murmur.

George looks out over the liquor.

The barman pours George a drink and
slides it over to him with a side of
disdain. George simply looks at it.
Slides a coin back to the barman. Then,
with a hint of sorrow, slides his drink
to

TARQUIN.

Tarquin frowns at the unexpected
kindness.

GEORGE
I'm guessing fish came before goats.

Tarquin looks at him with a bewildered
neolithic brow.

GEORGE
Do you still have your nets?

EXT/INT. SHED - NIGHT

Tarquin opens the two large doors of a
shed.

George goes inside first.

A few boats wrapped in cobwebs.

George walks towards a pile of nets.

Pulls at it, inspects it. Smiles.
That'll do.

EXT. LAKE - DAY

George is bent over a net in the middle
of the beach. He is securing medium
sized stones around the edge of the
net - much like a very large gladiators
net.

He looks sideways at his increasingly
large audience from the village,
spectating from a distance.

In front of the villagers huffs and puffs
Blasius, mortally offended in every
conceivable way, e marches towards
Albus and Sabra at the opposite end of
the beach.

Upon reaching Albus he spits as he gesticulates, unable to stand still. An itch he can't scratch.

BLASIUS
He's going to catch it?! And you... you...do they know you've negotiated their souls?!

ALBUS
Are you upset because you believe he will succeed?! Where's your faith in the goddess now Blasius?

Blasius opens his mouth, uncertain how to organize his words.

He looks at Sabra and opens his mouth wider as if asking her to come to his rescue. But Sabra however, keeps her eyes on George. Looks at the villagers. Narrows them before marching towards him.

Blasius's head pops forward like that of a turtle trying to beat the hare. He turns to Albus and hisses.

BLASIUS
These are souls not to be traded and sold. They will know of your plan to baptize them!

Albus reciprocates a threatening whisper.

ALBUS
Do so, and I will offer you myself to your lady of the lake.

Instantly feeling the sting, Blasius
steps backwards before turning and
running.

Sabra approaches George and immediately
sets to task to help George secure the
stones, which surprises him. She speaks
without looking up.

SABRA
I run when I should be staying... and
stay when I should run.

She smiles without looking at him.

Tarquin and his friends arrive with
horses, dragging long tree logs for the
villagers to sit on.

EXT. LAKE OF SILENE - LATER

George is standing at one end of the
beach, just inside the bush.
He fastens a rope to Ashkelon. The rope
extends to the top of a young palm
tree. The net sits right at the top of
the tree.

George pulls Ashkelon away from the
beach, so that the palm tree creaks
down towards down them, procuring the
function of catapult for the net.
Sabra stands nearby, and although her
arms are folded she's as bright and
curious as a kitten. She doesn't notice
George smiling at her.

George reaches a line drawn in the sand
- one of nine from previous attempts -
and stops.

He flicks the knot loose and the palm
tree, acting like a catapult, throws
the net towards the beach.

Dozens of villager eyes follow the net,
like some giant mobile spiders-web, it
chops through the air.

The net lands hard, right in front of
the

SACRIFICIAL STAKE

Some of the villagers applaud but it
quickly fizzles with the glares from
those still opposed to George and his
scheme.

Sabra suddenly notices George's eyes
on her and immediately straightens her
dress with discomfort, then drops her
shoulders at her own awkwardness.

GEORGE
You really don't want to see me dressed
up as a woman.

SABRA
You just can't ask properly, can you?

She walks away leaving George alone
with his smile.

EXT. LAKE - LATER

Tarquin stands with Ashkelon. The tree
and net reloaded. The trembling village
audience have moved further back and
hidden themselves in the brush.
Sabra stands at the sacrificial stake.
Touching it she notices it is looser
than before.

She looks sideways at George up at the
top trying to dislodge his spear still
stuck at the top of the tree by throwing
stones at it.

He growls. Gives up and hurries back
down.

He reaches Sabra and looking at the
lake draws his sword.

GEORGE
Always this time of day. Why?
Sabra wiggles the stake.

SABRA
I'll ask it. When it comes.

He looks at her as if noticing her
attractiveness for the first time.

GEORGE
You said 'it'?

She looks back at him.

GEORGE
'It'?

George breaks his reflective stupor and
shuffles awkwardly.

GEORGE
Yesterday it was... 'she'.

Uncomfortably he removes the few leaves
off the sleeve of her dress.

GEORGE
Just saying, she... it must be hungry
by now.

She frowns at his sudden awkwardness
and taps his hand away.

GEORGE
Who would have thought, gods get
hungry.

They look at each other as if for the
first time.

George turns and hurries away, hiding
behind the nearest tree.

The beach falls silent.

Sabra stands frowning, deep and alone
with her thoughts.

She looks sideways at George. Frowns
even more.

Shakes her head as if trying to think
of something else.

Looks up at the sky for help.

Nothing.

Looking out over the lake she sees it.

She.

The Dragon.

Only its eyes are visible. A little
more careful it looks right, looks
left, sees nothing.

Dips back out of sight.

Sabra swallows, her eyes bigger.

Steps back she feels the stake, it
moves with its looseness.

Enough to jog her courage, she
straightens herself. Even has time for
a stabbing glance in George's direction
for making her lapse.
This time the dragon is closer, but
still just its eyes visible.

Left, right, before fixing eyes on Sabra.

Again she swallows.

The Dragon glides closer.

Rising out of the water, it slowly
moves towards Sabra.

At the opposite end of the beach,
Tarquin rests his sword on the rope -
readying himself.

George, at the other end of the beach, mumbles.

GEORGE
Not yet Tarquin.

The Dragon steps closer but suddenly stops just before the net's landing spot.

It looks down at the sand. Sees the series of holes in the sand where the rocks had landed.

George behind the tree:

GEORGE
Come on you lazy lizard, a little closer.

The Dragon glares his liquid black eyes menacingly at Sabra.

Then sideways towards Tarquin. Doesn't see him but sees the bent over tree.

TARQUIN
She knows!

George takes the cross out of his tunic and silently storms the Dragon from behind the tree.

Tarquin slices the rope.

The net flies through the air.
George jumps up towards the dragon and slices his sword just as the dragon turns to face Sabra.

George's sword cuts into the Dragon's face.

With its alien shriek the Dragon rears.

As George falls back, the net falls right on top of him.

All sundry momentarily freeze, the Dragon tilts its head at these curious observations, before jolting its head towards its ultimate prize - Sabra.

George, tangled in the ropes, rips the cross off his neck and throws it with a shout to Sabra.

GEORGE
Sabra!

-- Her wide eyes move towards him. She catches the cross just as the Dragon bends over the top of her.

-- She holds up the cross.

-- Again the Dragon squeals at the sight of the cross, its curse reverberates the vertebrate to its core.

-- It turns its vehemence on George.

-- Astonished, Sabra looks at the cross, before throwing it back at George.

GEORGE
Run!

-- She doesn't. She turns to the sacrificial stake instead.

-- The cross lands in the sand next to George just as the Dragon puts his claw on George's chest.

-- Still inside the net George tries to reach for his cross - just a fingertip away.

-- Sabra has her arms around the stake and wiggles it loose with all her might.

-- The Dragon bends back its neck like some giant Cobra, ready for the final strike.

-- George cannot reach his cross. Looks the other side and sees his sword - closer.

-- The Dragon strikes...

-- Like lightning George grabs his sword and thrusts it upwards right into the Dragon's chin as she comes down for the bite.

-- George momentarily sees part of his sword in the Dragon's open mouth, pierced right through its tongue.

-- The now wounded beast pulls itself free from the sword as blood spurts from the Dragon's chin.

IN ONE STRAIGHT, RED, BLOODY, LINE

-- down George's face, chest and abdomen.

-- The Dragon comes in for the second strike and George has to think fast.

-- Still trapped inside the net, and with his bloody sword still in his grip, George pushes down a blood-stained horizontal imprint onto his own tunic...

COMPLETING THE FAMILIAR BLOODY CROSS

-- The Dragon recoils into the shallow water.

-- As he turns on Sabra, she manages to lift up the stake a little out of the ground, so that it drops backwards onto the nose of the beast.

-- This is enough to send the Dragon scurrying back in the water with a hissing roar.

-- Leaving a trail of mist, the beast vanishes.

-- Steam rising from the water as if the Dragon had been boiling.

-- George cuts himself from the net. Stands with heavy breath whilst looking out over the lake.

Sabra picks up his cross. Looks at it as if being hypnotized by it.

SABRA
This is your secret?

GEORGE
The Saviour's cross.

She turns in her hands like some
precious relic.

SABRA
Looks like your god beats my god after
all.

INT. LAKE - CONTINUOUS

The Dragon streaks through the water,
trailing blood like black ink.

EXT. LAKE - CONTINUOUS

Albus briskly approaches Sabra and
George.

ALBUS
He's wounded.

GEORGE/SABRA
She.

ALBUS
She...?

SABRA
It will be back...

GEORGE
...angrier.

Albus sees the red cross on George's
white tunic. Then the cross in Sabra's
hand.

GEORGE
You will honor our agreement?

Albus takes the cross from his daughter.
Inspects it. Mesmerized by like he's
just discovered an elixir.

ALBUS
Why don't you go home?

George takes it back from him.

ALBUS
Go home.

Albus turns to walk but George draws
his sword. The sharp metallic scrape
threatening.

GEORGE
We had an agreement.

Albus turns back to George, his voice
quietly sincere.

ALBUS
You will be remembered, for what you've
done here today. You will be remembered
for your courage.

Albus points at the cross in George's
hand.

ALBUS
But you have given us--

GEORGE
This is a mere symbol--

ALBUS
and means to protect ourselves--

GEORGE
we had an agreement--

ALBUS
ah the souls--

GEORGE
and their lives beyond this life.

Albus blinks.

GEORGE
We had an agreement.

ALBUS
We sometimes win, by losing.

Albus's words echo Diocletian's.

ALBUS/DIOCLETIAN
You are relieved.

Albus walks. George throws his sword in anger.

It whistles past Albus's head. Albus stops without looking at George.

ALBUS
Go home, George of Silene.

Continues.

GEORGE
I can't go home! You hear me?! Unless
you honor our agreement...I can't go
home!

George turns on Sabra.

GEORGE
Run woman! I ask you to run or I will
more than insult you!

Sabra looks at him fearlessly.
Sympathetically. Quietly.

SABRA
I must warn you, I just stood up to a
Dragon.

Sabra drifts her gaze to the net at
their feet.

She bends down to inspect it.

George growls at her before turning to
pace and kick up some sand.

GEORGE
Leave George. Go! What are you doing
here?!

SABRA (O.S.)
She knows this alcove.

George stops to listen to her. Sabra looks at her surroundings.

SABRA
Every tree and bush, she knows where they are.

Sabra looks at the erect palm tree they employed to be a catapult.

SABRA
She could see it bent over.

George points to the marks on the sand.

GEORGE
She saw the marks.

SABRA
Tree.

GEORGE
Marks!

Sabra digs her fingers into the sand.

SABRA
We can still catch her.

GEORGE
There is no--!

She stands suddenly. Their proximity closer. His final word softer. Much softer.

GEORGE
We. There's no--

She kisses him.

He looks at her, before kissing her back.

Water rises over them.

Still they kiss.

Slowly she pulls away from him.

Both their heads completely immersed in water.

Her head moves out of view.

George lies underneath the water gazing where she was moments ago.
He lifts his head...

OUT OF THE WATER

We see that he is...

LYING IN A WOODEN BATHTUB.

At the center of what looks like a bedroom.

George wipes the water from his face.

He hears the door click closed as if someone's just left his room.

He is visibly perturbed.

EXT. VILLAGE - DAY

George exits what looks like a primitive inn.

Walking towards the village square, he stops to take in his surroundings. The village appears desolate.

George sees crosses of every shape and size, tied, nailed, propped on every single home and shop front.

His face hardens.

The only person he sees is Blasius, standing at the entrance to his temple.

No cross visible.

After a venomous exchange, George turns and...

...bumps into Ashkelon - standing across his path.

GEORGE
Move mule. I'm finishing this.

George attempts to sidestep but again Ashkelon prevents him by taking a few hoofs forward.

Frown. Faint smile. Nod.

George accepts the invitation and gets on his horse.

Together they make their way down to the lake.

EXT. COUNTRY - CONTINUOUS

A burning village.

A few hundred Roman horsemen march down a concourse.

On either side of the concourse are crosses with the crucified dying on them.

Geralius in uniform and demonic expression, leads his soldiers.

EXT. LAKE OF SILENE - CONTINUOUS

Serenity descends on the beach of Silene.

Villagers like frozen spies peer from behind every variation of foliage.

From behind a tree George pensively watches...

...Sabra, who like some dutiful sentry, in front of the stake.

She touches George's cross, between her breasts where it rests, buried underneath her dress.

Watching the lake her steely eyes defiant.

George too looks out over the lake and whispers.

GEORGE
She's going to be angry.

The lake remains calm yet eerie.

In the distance George sees a slight ripple in the surface of the water.

The ripple turns into a wake.

George clenches his teeth.

GEORGE
Yep. She's livid.

-- The wake accelerates.

-- George looks behind him at Ashkelon, and a second horse tied to ropes that disappears into the sand.
-- Then at the opposite of the beach where two more horses are also tied to ropes.

-- George sees the Dragon's back spikes cutting through the water like a mountain range in rapid birth.

GEORGE
No.

-- His eyes bulge and like a bolt of lighting he sprints towards Sabra.

-- The Dragon shoots out the water as if being shot by the worlds most powerful crossbow.

-- Reaching Sabra, George dives to protect her.

-- Falls on top of her just as the beast glides past them.

-- All three hit the sand. The Dragon behind them.

-- In the distance Tarquin shouts.

-- Horses jolt forward, tightening and lifting the ropes buried in the sand to reveal

NETS

cupping up like giant clams.

-- Eight of them randomly buried on the beach.

-- A gamble; but one, luckily underneath the Dragon, cups upward and around, quickly entangling the creature.

-- The Dragon trapped, squirms and roars, it's tail lashing the sand around it.

-- George storms the Dragon with a roll of rope.

-- Lassoos the Dragon's mouth and jumps onto it.

-- Wraps and secures the rope around its mouth and pushes its head down onto the sand.

-- He hears a war-cry approaching and looks up to see...

TARQUIN AND THREE OTHERS APPROACHING

Armed with swords and pitchforks.

-- George's eyes widen.

-- He jumps off the Dragon who resumes its frenzy in trying to break free, but instead, gets more tangled inside the net.

-- George draws his own sword. Takes his stand between Tarquin, his horde and the Dragon.

-- Tarquin stops.

TARQUIN
Move aside.

GEORGE
She is mine to kill.

TARQUIN
Move aside!

-- Tarquin attacks by swinging his sword whilst two or three others round him to attempt to pierce the Dragon.

-- George blocks Tarquin kicks him full
in the chest.

-- Pulling up one of the nets, George
trips one.

-- Opens up the tunic of the second with
a single slice of his sword and blocks
the pitchfork of the third by clubbing
it down to the ground and then jumping
on it to snap it in half.

-- George and Tarquin rush each other,
swords locking, faces inches apart.
-- Tarquin the redder.

TARQUIN
Move aside!

GEORGE
Not until I get paid!

Tarquin pushes him away.

TARQUIN
For a smart man you're naively
optimistic.

His cronies laugh.

TARQUIN
We're not getting in the water with--

His words quickly peter as he sees
Sabra take George's side.

ALSO WITH A SWORD IN HER HAND.

She raises it. Ready. George smiles.

GEORGE
Oh. I think you are.

-- Tarquin attacks.

-- Sabra and George, back to back,
block and slice.

-- George sees the Dragon biting through
its ropes.

-- He reaches behind him and snatches
his cross off from around Sabra's neck.

-- Lunges for the Dragon and with a few
quick slices of his sword breaks all
the ropes - assisting in freeing the
Dragon.

-- Tarquin and cronies immediately
freeze their fighting, astonished at
what they are seeing.

-- Even the Dragon pauses in shock
surprise before...

-- ...George places his cross against
the Dragon's forehead - immediately
subduing the creature against its will.

-- The Dragon has no choice but to
closes its eyes.

-- Shut tight its body quivers with
suppressed fury.

-- Unlike Tarquin's, with eyes wide.

TARQUIN
It'll eat you first.

GEORGE
It might. It might not.

Tarquin backs away. Relaxes. Puts his
sword in the ground and sits down.
Indicating that he'll wait.

George and Sabra look at each other,
not certain what to do next, when...

De-doof, de-doof, de-doof!

All eyes shift to...

ASHKELON

-- ...stomping in like a demon horse,
straight for Tarquin and his men.

-- With snorts, spurts, neighs, rears,
tight circles, and flicking his long
black mane, Ashkelon's mayhem causes
Tarquin and his supporters to scurry
away like rats in front of a fire,
leaving behind all their weaponry.

-- George and Sabra see each other with
relief.

-- But just as quickly stiffen at the
slow hissing sound behind them - of a
patient Dragon...

-- ...for George still holds the cross
against the Dragon's forehead.

EXT. COUNTRYSIDE - CONTINUOUS

The roaring hooves of Geralius and his
troops.

Behind them, another burning village,
accessorized with the crucified.

EXT. SILENE - CONTINUOUS

The road to Silene is eerily quiet.

Suddenly there is a rustle amongst the
trees leading up from the lake.

Growing louder Ashkelon suddenly bursts
from the brush galloping like he's seen
a ghost.

George steps onto the road.
In his hand, a rope, with which he
pulls...

The Dragon...

It stumbles into the road.

The cross is firmly tied to its forehead,
preventing it from entirely opening its
eyes. Saliva hangs from the quivering
beast's clenched jaws. Formidable and
for now, forcibly tamed.

Sabra steps in beside the beast.

Looks curiously at the...

STEAM...
...rising from the creatures armored
skin.

Mesmerized, she touches it - and burns
her fingers.

SABRA
It's like she's heating up?

George stops at the end of the road that
enters the village and looks at Sabra.

SABRA
I have... belief...

She touches her chest and looks at it
as if she's never noticed it before.

SABRA
Inside.

But I also have unbelief.

They are side by side.

GEORGE
It doesn't go away.

I did not rise to my belief.

That's why I ran.

Sabra looks out over her Village.

SABRA
And this is where you stopped. To prove
wrong your cowardice.

She looks at him.

SABRA
I'd say you've succeeded, George of
Nicomedia.

He at her.

EXT. SILENE COUNTRYSIDE

Geralius pulls in the reigns of his
horse.

Behind him, a mass of Roman horsemen.

In between the horsemen we see..

SUPERNATURAL SKELETAL RIDERS IN GREEN
ROBES.

In the distance...

THE LAKE OF SILENE

The smoke trials of the village.

Like some frenzied land shark Geralius
kicks his horse back into gear.

EXT. VILLAGE OF SILENE - DAY

Ashkelon, George, Sabra and the Dragon
enter the village square.

George ties the Dragon around one of the
pillars in the center of the square.

He takes in his surroundings. Sees the
crosses on the doors.

He sees a door slam shut.

Another window closes with a creak.

George roars.

GEORGE
Sileneeeee!

Silence.

GEORGE
We had an agree--

Whoop-whoop-whoop! Thwak!
An arrow hits George in the shoulder.

GEORGE
Aargh!

He falls to one knee. Puts his hand
around the arrow.

Tarquin appears with his bow. Reloads.

Sabra puts herself between he and
George.

Tarquin still aims his bow.

TARQUIN
He's not one of us!

SABRA
No he's not!

But he's better than us!

Blasius touches his heart in his
fairytale manner.

George pulls out the arrow with a
groan, stands back up and eyes Tarquin
with menace.

SABRA
George, has brought us a better way. I
can't speak for all...

She looks at Blasius.

SABRA
...but I want to live.

Albus arrives on his horse, jumps down
to stands with George and his daughter.

Tarquin immediately drops his bow with
clenched teeth.

Curiosity opens village doors and
windows as villagers appear to see
their leader speak.

Albus begins his piercing gaze on
Blasius.

ALBUS
Our gods do not care for us!

Albus points at the Lizard beast.

ALBUS
If they did, they would not send us
Dragons!

He beats his chest.

ALBUS
I, for one, will follow any god that
pursues me.

And I feel...

...pursued!

And if a better way means I wash
myself, I bat...

Looks at George.

GEORGE
Baptize.

ALBUS
Baptize myself, then that is what I
shall do.

As more villagers approach the center
square, Albus Looks at Tarquin.

ALBUS
I gave this man my word.

TARQUIN
You spoke for us my Lord.

ALBUS
That, I did.

But I shan't order. I will ask. Will
you join me?

Villagers look at each other.
Suddenly...

A CLAP

One person applauding. Slow and
deliberate.

Geralius walks into the village square,
applauding with characteristic disdain.

His soldiers rumble in on horse and
foot and quickly surround the entire
village square.

Geralius calmly draws his sword and
immediately runs Albus through.

Coarse and wild, Sabra screams.

George, stupefied, holds her.

Geralius hisses in the ear of Albus.

GERALIUS
Do not lead your people astray.

Drops him on the stones.

Like one man Roman soldiers draw their
swords.

Like some new proprietor having acquired
an estate, Geralius paces, drinking in
its audience, but stops when he sees
the crosses on the doors. Sneers.

Sabra falls on her knees weeping over
her father.

Geralius turns to inspect the Dragon.
Sees the cross tied onto its forehead.

GERALIUS
So why haven't you killed it?

GEORGE
Because you tend to have the
unfortunate disposition of interfering.

GERALIUS
Intervening.

Geralius calmly puts his sword point
against the Dragon's head.

GERALIUS
'Geralius, Dragon slayer'. A nice ring
to it, don't you think?

Geralius turns his head to accommodate
a realization.

GERALIUS
You need the Dragon to bargain for the
souls of these pagans.

Geralius turns to his village audience
and raises his voice.

GERALIUS
Be baptized and I will slay your
Dragon! Is that what he told you? Is
that the bargain?

Then go! Go down to the water. Wash
yourselves clean!

Go!

No one moves. Geralius feigns surprise.

GERALIUS
No-one? Not even one?

He turns to face George with contempt.

GERALIUS
You could not even manage one?

Suddenly pulls him closer and runs his
sword through George's side - a wound.

Two soldiers grab George as he twists
with pain.

GERALIUS
With just enough blood to see your own
head fall in Nicomedia.

Geralius triumphantly sheathes his
sword.

Like a lioness Sabra bounds on Geralius,
only to meet his fist which like a giant
boulder knocks her out cold.

George falls to his knees, trying to
both stop the bleeding and go to Sabra,
but is held back by the two soldiers.

Geralius looks down at Sabra.

GERALIUS
Congratulations.
You managed one.

Looks at dead Albus.

GERALIUS
And that must be number two?

GEORGE
You would not have honored our
agreement.

GERALIUS
Are you a seer?--

GEORGE
--because you are not yet a man.

Geralius laughs.

GERALIUS
That's all you have?

Mimics George's last comment.

GERALIUS
'I'm not yet a man?' Is that it? Is
that all you have?!

GEORGE
It is because... you weigh... nothing.

Geralius becomes theatrical like he's
understanding some grand epiphany.

GERALIUS
Oh... it's 'My god is bigger than your
god'. Again?

Geralius puts his mouth against George's
ear and whispers.

GERALIUS
There are no gods! How do you think
we control the Rabelaisian? You should
have kept running.

George suddenly grabs Geralius by his
armor and hisses back.

GEORGE
We are all called to face the Dragon!
And I...
will...
slay...
you!

The soldiers drag George off Geralius,
who appears a little more shaken.

Geralius looks down at Sabra, then at
the cross on the Dragon. His flippancy
dissipated.

GERALIUS
The symbol of contention.

Sees steam rise from the Dragon's skin,
more so than before.

GERALIUS
Very well...

He puts his sword between the ropes
securing the cross.

GERALIUS
...let's see how much your God cares?

The soldiers and everyone back away
leaving Sabra alone in front of the
beast.

GEORGE
Nooo!

-- Geralius, wearing gloves, takes the
cross in one hand and sword in the
other, cuts the ropes.

-- The Dragon's quivering stops.

-- Its eyes fly open. Each black eye
fills with fire.

-- Still holding up the cross, Geralius
retreats with a smile, leaving Sabra in
front of the Dragon.

-- The Dragon roars, shaking the tiles
off the village roofs.

-- Opens its mouth and...

BREATHES FIRE!

-- The heat and noise above Sabra
is enough to shake her back into
consciousness.

-- She sits up but is immediately
scooped up by one of the Dragon's wings.
Neatly and securely rolled up inside.

-- George roars above the din.

-- Still clutching the wound in his
side, soldiers grab him and tie up his
wrists.

-- George sees Sabra's eyes, no longer filled with courage and defiance, but terror. He watches her scream swallowed in the mayhem.

-- Like a giant alligator, the Dragon slithers its way through the village, discharging fire into the homes either side.

-- The fire quickly spreads.

-- George struggles with the rope around his wrists which are tied to one of the soldier's saddles.

-- The soldiers quickly form their ranks, with Geralius at the head.

-- The Dragon disappears out of view in the direction of the lake, steam pouring upward from its skin.

-- Geralius gives George a triumphant smile before securing his helmet and setting the march out of the burning village.

-- Defeated, George is dragged along.

-- Behind him, villagers scurry with water buckets in the Sisyphean task of putting out the ferocious blaze.

EXT. ROAD TO SILENE - CONTINUOUS

The road is quiet.

The wind brushes through the trees.

A soft rumble in the soil.

Geralius and his small army march along
the road that crescents the beach.

Raising his arm, he brings his company
to a halt.

He watches the Dragon, with Sabra under
its bat-like-wing, bending bush and
tree to get to the lake, with puffs of
flame and smoke shooting into the air.

Halfway along the company line, George
too watches, in helpless horror.

George drops to his knee, as tears and
blood fall to the ground.

Geralius smiles at George's brokenness,
and shouts.

GERALIUS
It means to baptize her!

The company roars with laughter.

George pulls his iron cross out from
inside his shirt.

Touches it tenderly.

Drops his head and closes his eyes.

All other sounds fading.

Ridicule turns to echoes, laughter into
warped sounds.

George hears his own breath and the soft rushing of the wind.

In his anguish he mumbles a hollow prayer.

GEORGE
Let me begin again.

The wind blows louder...

De-doof, de-doof, de-doof...

George's eyes fly open.

All eyes shift to the opposite bank to the beach.

ASHKELON...

-- Charges down directly towards the horse that's got the rope tied to George.

-- Headbutt-crashes straight into the side of the saddle.

-- The soldier crashes down onto the ground, right in front of George.

-- Simultaneously, and as the soldier tries to get to his feet, George's

SPEAR

-- Lodged in the branches above, falls like a bolt of lightning from Zeus

right into the soldier's neck, killing
him instantly.

-- George looks up at the trees,
branches flaying in the accelerated wind.

-- With renewed vigor George unsheathes
the dead soldier's sword and cuts
himself free with one slice.

-- Pulls out the spear from the dead
soldier and helicopters it over his
head, knocking down two attacking
soldiers off their own horses.

-- He charges a third, running him
through.

-- This time Geralius mimics his own
horror.

GERALIUS (O.S.)
Stop him!

-- George jumps on Ashkelon and takes a
last look at the Dragon slithering into
the water.

His eyes shift to the

ROCKY CLIFF

...protruding across a third of the
lake.

-- Bewildered soldiers swirling around
him.

-- George pats Ashkelon neck, leans
towards his ears and whispers.

GEORGE
You started this. You have to finish it
Ashkelon.

Let's see how much you weigh.

-- Geralius charges whilst George blocks
a sword and pierces another.

-- He quickly drags the soldier from
his horse pulling him across Ashkelon's
saddle.

-- Does the same with a second soldier
dragging him on top of the first.

-- Then a third, packing Ashkelon with
weight.

-- Then charges Geralius.

-- From Geralius's point of view: only
George's head is visible behind the
pile-up of three dead soldiers on his
saddle.

-- Geralius's horse stumbles against
the bank as George charges past,
immediately crushing his leg against a
rock. He falls in agony from his horse.

-- George gallops at full speed for the
protruding ledge.

-- He sees the Dragon's fins disappear
below the water.

-- Spurs Ashkelon to accelerate.

-- This formidable animal sweats under
the weight of four men.

-- They turn onto the ledge.

-- Full speed.

-- Time slows down.

-- George reaches the edge and pulls
Ashkelon up for the jump.
-- His grip tightens around his spear.

-- Soldiers and villagers like ice
sculptures watch George and his horse
Ashkelon slice the air in slow motion.

-- Geralius's screams inaudibly red.

-- Tarquin stands wide-eyed on the
beach.

-- George and Ashkelon, with all the
weight of the dead, cut into the lake
like a meteor.

-- Swallowed.

-- Vanished.

-- Silence...

...as the wind retreats.

INT. LAKE - CONTINUOUS

-- George and Ashkelon sink. The bubble

trails straight and furious.

-- As if Hades is woken, the murky
darkness encroaches eerily around them.
George again grips his spear tighter.

-- The soldiers bodies loosen and drift
out.

-- Ashkelon, struggling with breath,
swallows water, starts kicking to turn
himself upwards, to no avail.

-- Nearing the bottom of the Lake,
George gently pats his horse...

-- ...as Ashkelon jerks his final
moments.

-- George is suddenly rushed and
thrashed by the Dragon shooting past.

-- The water makes George's movements
sluggish but he manages to thrust his
spear upwards.

-- The spear hooks into the creatures'
wing, opposite to the wing still curled
around Sabra.

-- Managing to hold unto his spear,
George is dragged through the water
underneath the beast.

-- He catches a glimpse of Sabra,
staring wide-eyed at him from inside the
opposite wing - life rapidly leaking
from her.

-- The Dragon bends its neck around to snap at George.

-- George grips the wing, pulls out the spear and thrusts it again, this time down through the neck.

-- The Dragon's muffled shriek shakes the water.

-- Its wings stretch open from the piercing.

-- Sabra falls, her eyes closing.

-- George swims for her, catches her, and drags her up to the surface, whilst...

-- The Dragon rocks in a frenzied recoil to try and get to the spear stuck through its neck.

-- Catching a glimpse of George reaching the surface, the Dragon makes one final pursuit...

EXT. BEACH - CONTINUOUS

-- Anxious villagers and soldiers dot the beach.

-- They see the water bubble.

Then silence.

-- George suddenly burst through the surface, stands quickly pulling an unconscious Sabra out of the water.

-- Behind him the Dragon rises. Spear through its neck.

-- George let's Sabra go, faces the Dragon as it comes down for the bite.

-- As the Dragon's jaws snap in front of George's face, he grabs the spear, turns it and thrusts it into the sand, pinning down its head.

-- Its body squirms, its tail lashes, but George holds the spear with all of his strength.

-- He looks sideways at Sabra. Her face the same as that of his dead mother that once lay in the fountain.

-- Whispers inside his head.

GEORGE
Sabra.

Wake up Sabra.

-- Immediately she coughs up water and breathes.

-- George tightens his hold on the snapping Dragon, each tiring out the other.

-- Finally the beast dies, and sink into the shallow water.

George rushes over to Sabra floating in the water, blood seeping from her stomach.

Her cold white face looking up at his.

SABRA
George...

She grips his shirt.

Her life slipping away rips apart his
gaze as he leans towards her.

Her voice quietly coarse.

SABRA
I want to begin again.

With oceans crashing inside his eyes,
George whispers.

GEORGE
Sabra of Silene...your sins are
forgiven.

George pushes her underneath the
water...

...and watches her eyes close.

His own tears unstoppable.

George sees two ghosts appear beside
Sabra - His own mother and father look
at him and smile, like they did so
often when he was a boy. Together they
accompany Sabra's ghost, vanishing into
the depths of the lake.

George stands.

Defeated.

Heroically grim inside Sabra's watery grave.

His head hangs for a long while.

Geralius steps onto the beach. With teeth showing and sword drawn, he limps into the water.

But quickly he is overtaken by villagers also making their way into the water.

Geralius slows down until he eventually stops.

He watches what seems to be the entire village wading into the water towards George.

George looks up and sees the villagers of Silene coming towards him.

Tarquin the first to reach him.

His two consorts close behind carry Sabra's body out of the water.

Tarquin, facing George, takes off his coat. Discards it in the water.

The burly man looks down at the water and crosses his arms over his chest.

George looks past him.

All the other villagers approach with the arms crossed. Almost all are wearing crosses.

George puts his hand on Tarquin's shoulder. His lips move. Tarquin nods. George pushes him backwards underneath the water.

On the beach Geralius shouts (inaudibly) at his hesitant soldiers to stop what is happening.

Tarquin rises from the water. George embraces him.

The next villager, a woman, steps forward.

In the distance we see the smoke, burning what was once the village of Silene.

EXT. NICOMEDIA - DAY

The Imperial city of Nicomedia. Sprawling and brilliant.

From above, its citizens rush towards the central square.

Erected is a platform.

On it stands a man dressed in black and a black hood covers his head. A familiar axe rests in his hands.

In front of him stands George. Beside him ten other men. Hands tied.

George looks up at the balconies.

Sees Geralius.

TITLE CARD:

-- In 302 AD Geralius issued an edict that Christians be persecuted and executed. Even if they were soldiers of Rome. Allegiances were tested by enforcing public sacrifices to Roman gods.

George sees Diocletian. Beside him, ALEXANDRA his wife, a veil covering her face.

TITLE CARD:

-- Alexandra, the wife of Diocletian, becomes a convert to Christianity.

She turns and runs inside.

George looks at peace as he walks to where he is to place his head.

The axeman lifts his ax.

TITLE CARD:

-- George was decapitated on the 23 April 303 AD.

It goes black just as the axe falls.

TITLE CARD:
-- Eight years later, Geralius ended
the Christian persecution in 311 AD.

THE END

Made in the USA
Middletown, DE
31 August 2021